The

Log Cabin

Gas Station

Also by Hal D. Simpkin

G-Eye

The

Log Cabin

Gas Station

Hal D. Simpkin

**Published by Mira Digital Press
Brentwood, Missouri**

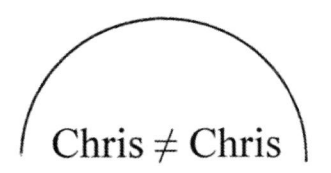

Chris ≠ Chris

A Chris-Chris.LLC book

Copyright © 2012 by Hal D. Simpkin. All rights reserved.

Published by Mira Digital Press, U.S.A. No part of this publication may be reproduced, stored in a retrieval system or transmitted in any form without the prior written permission of the author.

This is a work of fiction. Events, places, characters and names are either products of the author's imagination or are used fictitiously and are not to be interpreted as real. Any resemblance to actual events, locales, institutions, business establishments or persons, living or dead, is coincidental.

First printing
1 2 3 4 5 6 7 8 9 10

Cover design by Mira Digital Press.

ISBN: 978-0-9859778-8-7

Chrissie: warm smiles and strength.

ACKNOWLEDGEMENTS

Chris Simpkin
Editor Extraordinaire

Bob Fleetwood
Bob Garthe
Michele Beger
Critical Reviews and Contributions

Mary Lou Veytia
Linguistics

Pat Grace
Contents Consultant

EPISODES

For The Want of a Fuse	1
Emil	11
Lucius	29
Gypsies	51
Watch Out for the Cheater	69
Pike's Pond	89
Bill	103
The Tail of the Little Gray-Haired Lady	113
These Foolish Things	121
Partying is Such Sweet Sorrow	139

FOR
THE WANT
OF
A FUSE

*Chris learns that while a good deed may be a good thing,
it is still best to bloom where one is planted.*

FOR THE WANT OF A FUSE

It had been another hot June day. Business was slow. When they could, folks were staying at home, in front of the fan, or in the shade—anywhere but in the hot car. In the Log Cabin Gas Station, things were hardly better.

"Log Cabin," the name of the place was not fanciful. The only building on the premises once had been someone's log home. Now it was someone's gas station.

Out front ran the old rock road. The Rock Road had always existed to join the St. Louis area with St. Charles, Missouri, once, the state capital. It was rough, muddy, and rocky, but the horses never seemed to mind. Lately however, motorcars had all but replaced the horses. The final resident of the cabin watched from his front door the gradual building of automobile traffic.

That resident, whose name is now lost, reasoned during his middle years that it might make sense—instead of going into the city to earn a living—to stay home and let the business come to him. He hired some help and had gas pumps installed between his house and the road. Soon, the business grew. When he'd had enough, he sold it to another entrepreneur and took himself back to the farm.

The entrepreneur d' jour owned a number of similar businesses and hired help at all of them. Chris Christopher, needing a summer job, found it at the Log Cabin Gas Station.

As to comfort, the best that could be said would be that the place held the heat well.

Albert had ridden by around noon, to mooch a soda and visit with Chris. He had a knack for being able to predict the times when Chris wouldn't be real busy. They would sit inside, or on the split log in front of the cabin, depending on the weather. Albert would talk at length, telling events of his day that he was certain Chris would find interesting. When Chris tired of trying to make sense of what he was hearing, he'd hand Albert another pop from the cooler. When business called Chris, Albert would quietly ride off. Today, *he* had other business and left after about a half hour.

Albert had been—apparently from birth—stricken by some malady that had left him less than bright and with a facial deformity that caused the young man to have a drooping lower lip. The lip malformation resulted in Albert's constant drooling.

It was difficult to understand Albert's speech.

Fate seemed to compensate Albert by providing him with an exceptional physique. At about six feet tall, his shoulders were broad and muscular, his waist trim and firm. His legs were powerful. Doubtlessly contributing to the maintenance of his physical shape, Albert rode a bicycle everywhere he went.

Albert idolized Chris. He was his loyal friend.

Getting on toward evening, a convertible version of the latest model Mercury automobile pulled—top down—onto the station lot, stopping in the wide area near the entrance to the building. This approach usually signaled a cigarette or soda pop purchase, an occasional request for help with directions, or—not often—a request for help with an automotive problem.

Through the front window, Chris watched the driver climb out and head for the open door of the log cabin. He met him at the door and issued a large Customer-Meeting smile. "Hi, how can I help you?"

"I need to ask you to replace a headlight fuse. I noticed last evening that the headlights weren't working. I was able to get home before dark. Problem now is, I have no idea where the fuses go. But I imagine you do."

"I imagine I don't," Chris gave him a wry smile. "What I don't know about cars would fill Wellston's library. I drive a Model-A Ford...the one parked over there against the fence. It has no headlight fuse at all."

"Oh boy, I've got trouble." Chin down, the customer shook his head nervously. "I'm on my way to pick up my date and it's getting dark." He paused. "Do you think you could help me find that fuse?" As an afterthought, he added, "I really don't need to get dirty."

Chris was not in a magnanimous frame of mind. Earlier in the day his lunch had been interrupted by the arrival of a customer during a normally slow period of the afternoon. After a fill-up, he wanted his oil checked, the windshield washed, the rear wheels tire pressure measured and detailed instructions for locating a lumber yard that was just down the street. Finally rid of the customer, back inside the office, Chris discovered he had left his lunch box open. The contents had been spread on the desk and were being eaten by a scraggly stray dog that wandered in from the heat of the afternoon. Chris plucked the dog from the seat of his chair and shooed him out the front door.

But Chris was usually a good-natured and forgiving guy; he tried to take such things in stride. Now he was trying to be patient with another customer whose needs and wants were pushing the limit of reason.

Chris had already eyed the young man's duds: light-colored seersucker pants, white linen jacket, brown-and-white saddle shoes. "Usually all I do is pump gas," but—after a deep breath—"I'll see what I can do." The driver was visibly relieved.

Chris walked toward the car. Over his shoulder, he cautioned his customer. "I'll look around. Wait here, but whatever you do don't touch anything. There's dirt and oil everywhere." The driver stopped in his tracks.

Opening the driver's door, Chris rolled onto his back, slid from the seat onto the floor so he could see under the dashboard. He saw nothing that resembled a fuse—good or blown. He wriggled out of the car.

"No luck." Walking around, he entered the passenger-side, looked into the glove compartment. No fuses.

Shaking his head in the direction of his customer, Chris got out and stood, head down, thinking. Nothing came to mind. Disappointed, he looked back at the driver and saw growing concern.

"Is it possible they could have put fuses in the trunk?"

"Hell, I'll try anywhere," Chris answered without enthusiasm. "Would you unlock it, please?"

The driver did and Chris looked. To no avail.

Then Chris remembered a 1920s vintage Oakland automobile. One night, a couple of years earlier, he and a friend who was the owner of the Oakland had found a fuse panel under the car, attached to the frame below the driver's door. Aha! Maybe.

Chris swung open the driver's door. He lay down on his back, reaching under the car. He grasped the frame below the door and pulled himself through the chat rock far enough to see the bottom of the car and the frame.

By this time the sun had set. Visibility was poor. He called to the driver, "Do you have a flashlight in the car?"

"Dammit, no, I'm sorry, I don't."

"Okay, I have one in the center drawer of my desk. How about you go get it and hand it to me?" Chris did not want to slide back out across those rocks until he was finished looking for a fuse under the car.

"I've got it." Calling from the door of the log cabin, the driver headed back toward the car.

At that moment began a chain of horrific events.

A sudden gust of evening breeze caught the driver's door. The large, heavy door swung closed, smashing the tips of three fingers on each of Chris' hands.

The Log Cabin Gas Station

Chris screamed in pain.

The driver, seeing what had happened, rushed to help. He swung the car door open. In the beam of the flashlight the man saw blood and mangled fingertips. He recoiled, knuckles pressed to his lips. "Oh my God."

Into this scene of horror rode Albert, his bright bicycle-light illuminating the area. Albert saw his good friend Chris on the ground, clearly in pain and bleeding. A stranger with an object in his hand was bending over Chris.

From under the car, Chris caught a vision of the nightmare that was about to begin. Albert dismounted.

Chris screamed, "No Albert, no Albert, no!" He went unheard.

Albert struck like a bolt of summer lightning. He grabbed the man's collar—violently pulled him away from Chris.

The man staggered backward, almost recovered his balance, tripped on the edge of the oil pit behind him. With arms flailing, he fell into the filthy, scum-covered water.

Chris struggled to his knees on the chat-rock driveway and watched Albert reach down with one arm. Calm now, Albert plucked the driver from the pit and deposited him onto the ground.

In shock, silently staring ahead, the dripping-wet driver, moving like an automaton with only one goal, slogged his way into his car, got it started and drove away—without benefit of headlights—into the darkness, westbound on the Rock Road.

Albert helped Chris into the office. Chris used his left, least-damaged hand to phone Frank's house.

Ila answered the phone. Yes, both Tommy and Dean were home. They would be there in a couple of minutes. Arriving in separate cars, Tom drove Chris to the County Hospital while Dean covered at the gas station.

Chris never saw nor heard of the Mercury driver again. He counted that blessing silently.

Some time later a fellow, more knowledgeable about Mercurys than Chris was, told him: "That model of Mercury had circuit breakers instead of fuses in the headlight circuit."

"Oh."

EMIL

*Chris witnesses the power of
well-meant kindness and
unavoidable social pressure.*

EMIL

Emil was a drunk, a bum, a friendly neighbor, and a man with a remarkable history. The first three adjectives were obvious upon inspection. That he was truly remarkable could be learned during those times when he came sober into the Log Cabin Gas Station. Nonetheless, a sober visit might occur at some peril to one's appetite. Emil almost always stunk of sweat...who knows how old? And of yesterday's alcohol.

Emil was a man of moderate height—probably five-six or five-seven. His build was trim and athletic, suggesting that of a lightweight fighter. He had a square-shaped head, blond hair and blue wide-set eyes. When he was in decent shape he frequently showed a pleasant smile. His speech was tinted with a noticeable Germanic accent. When sober, his walk suggested a military background. When he had been drinking he tended to drag his left foot slightly as he walked.

The fellow was remarkably well-informed for a rather young man. Chris guessed him to be in his mid-to-late 30s. Occasionally, when Emil was sober, or nearly sober, recently bathed and in relatively clean clothes, Chris found the man to be good company. He spoke knowledgeably on a wide range of subjects. Chris recognized Emil as someone he could learn from and Emil appreciated that.

Emil's sobriety or sanitary condition notwithstanding, Chris was ready to welcome, or at least accept, his drop-in visits during a day at the station.

Chris was in the middle of his second summer of work at the Log Cabin Gas Station. He was a graduate of Normandy High School, in the block just west of the station. Chris spent most of his summer vacation earning money for his continued education. At age 19 he was by this time one of the more experienced employees of the station. In September, he would begin his second year at Rupert-Glispe University in Decatur, Illinois. He was working on a B.S. degree in business management.

A good-looking young man, he was trim of stature and just a little under six feet tall.

His dark hair and ability to sing got him occasional evening jobs with local bands. High-school girls often compared him to Frank Sinatra; he usually rated a close but definite second.

Chris owned a 1928 Model A Ford—a coupe with a rumble seat—yet another definite advantage for a sociable guy. He was friendly, outgoing and a bit of a wisecracker.

It was another hot sweaty day. At noon the temperature was holding fast at 95° with no breeze. Gas pumping business had been markedly slow this morning; folks were avoiding driving. At least the dust from the chat-rock driveway had little to blow it around—that is unless a car did happen to drive in. The huge cottonwoods that overhung the log cabin from their position in the lot north of the building did little to provide shade from the afternoon sun.

Hungry at lunch time, Chris brought back a pulled-pork sandwich from the inn next door. He transformed the office desk into a lunch table. No sooner was the brown-paper grocery sack opened when Emil strolled across the parking lot, heading for the office. Chris held his breath, both literally and figuratively.

Old buddy, I hope you have had a bath.

Luck was holding out. Emil was indeed rather clean, with fairly-fresh clothes.

"Hey, Emil, how's it going? Lunchtime. Here, have a soda pop on me." Chris extended a hand with a nickel enclosed. Emil accepted the treat, dropped the nickel into the cooler's coin-slot, extracted a pineapple soda and sat on the side chair. He watched as Chris began to eat his sandwich.

"I suggest you drink a glass of water before you eat that," was Emil's unsolicited comment.

Chris sent his eyes right, raised his right eyebrow. "Why?"

Emil was happy to answer. "Always a good idea—even more important when the food might be hard to digest.

"Also, don't drink water with food in your mouth." Emil furnished an afterthought.

"Yeah—why?" Chris was only somewhat interested.

"Interferes with the action of the salivary glands."

"Right?" Chris shot a skeptical look in Emil's direction.

Emil appeared not to notice; he continued his lecture. "It's okay to drink a sip or two after each swallow."

"Where'd you learn that?"

Emil took a deep breath, held it, released it as a long sigh, and began his answer. "Chris, in the Army of Germany, before and during the war, I was a medical doctor."

Chris shook his head, his eyes blinked. "You are...is that right?"

Emil nodded.

"How, how did...?" Chris tilted his head, squinted slightly, began again. "How did you get to be here?"

"I was taken prisoner by General Patton and brought to a Missouri detention camp. By the time the war ended I had been working for a while on the farm of a man near Potosi. Some of us prisoners were given an opportunity to keep our jobs and work to become citizens. Of course I accepted the opportunity. Later I was married to the owner's sister."

"Really? I didn't know you're married."

"No more. She left me...could not stand the drinking."

Chris genuinely liked Emil. He sat quiet, thinking about the story he just heard. "That's too bad. I'm sorry that all happened."

Emil, reflecting, nodded his head and said nothing. He got up slowly. "Thanks, Chris, for the soda." He left the building, headed in the direction of home.

The unmistakable ticka-ticka-ticka of the Model T exhaust broke up Chris' mid-day forty winks. He looked up from his desk in time to see his great-uncle Charley Becker's ancient car roll up to the gas pumps. His uncle remained seated in the car for a while as he performed some manipulations therein. The engine produced two sharp backfire reports and then stopped. The driver got out slowly, turned, smiled and offered his left hand to Chris who had extended his own right hand to shake.

The portly man tilted his head, looked sadly at Chris. "I'm sorry Chris...the rheumatism is bad today. I can barely move this right arm to shake like a gentleman." Then, "I'd like to go in and use your restroom—if I may.

"Put a little gas in her...will you, boy?"

"Yes, sir, Dicke Beck." Chris placed his right hand on his uncle's shoulder in lieu of a handshake and turned toward the car. Mr. Becker turned and headed briskly for the office.

Chris lifted the car seat to expose the gas tank. He removed the twist-off cap and measured the tank's fuel level, using the graduated wooden stick he found on the floor. He inserted the pump-hose nozzle, filled the Model T's tank with Regular.

By the time Chris had pumped gasoline, wiped the windshield and performed a quick walk-around, he saw that his uncle had bought a couple of pops. One bottle in each hand, the old man stood at the door to hand one to Chris. "Thank you, Dicke Beck."

Dicke—a German word connoting fat—was appended to part of his last name. The uncle had composed the name as a special gift for Chris when he was a very young child. Now a young man, Chris enjoyed continuing to use it and clearly the old man enjoyed it himself.

They sat in the office. Chris had the small side chair, the uncle took the more comfortable chair behind the desk. In a few moments Mr. Becker had introduced the subject of conversation for this visit. It was to be the continuing shortage of some commodities. Although the war was more than two years in the past, the "incompetent lousy pups who we taxpayers are feeding to get the job done" needed to be exposed.

Throughout his oration, the uncle was emphasizing his point by gesticulating actively with first one arm and then the other. Chris was gratified to see that his uncle's right arm had substantially healed, probably due to the medicinal effects of the Coca-Cola he was drinking.

Chris loved his Uncle Dicke Beck and looked forward to this traditional performance whenever the two of them got together.

At this moment, Emil entered the station. Emil was not having a good day. He had been drinking but was not drunk. He had been sweating and had not washed up. He was ripe.

Now...Charley Becker was a working man. He had worked, and worked around, working men, all his working life. He was not surprised—nor was he particularly put off—by Emil's condition. But he could not identify with it. Charley, on the other hand, was a man who kept himself clean—he was a man's man and a gentleman. Having his choice, he would have preferred the company of a more well-kempt man than this Emil to whom he had just been introduced. Nonetheless, he greeted Emil cordially and even shook hands agilely enough, having just undergone a sort of miracle cure.

The two men seemed to recognize their ancestral backgrounds-in-common and exchanged a few sentences in German. Chris, having grown up with the German language spoken regularly in his own home, was able to keep track of the thread of the conversation...the weather, the economy and...

When that conversation was exhausted, Chris—in English now—gave his uncle a condensed description of Emil's history. Becker found the story to be interesting and told him so. Emil seemed pleased, then, soon after took his leave.

Just the two of them again, the uncle counseled his nephew. "Boy, you need to say something to your friend. He has a BO problem."

Chris frowned. "How can I say anything about that?"

"You owe it to him as a friend and as a man." Chris thought about that, then smiled. "Maybe I could hand him a cake of Lifebuoy soap as a hint."

"Well maybe...but say something kind and firm when you do it, you understand?"

"Yes, sir."

Changing the subject, Chris asked about the Model T. That topic reminded the uncle of something else that was stuck in his craw: "Let me tell you what some smart- aleck copper said to me yesterday. He had the nerve to walk up to me as I was getting into my car in a legal parking spot. He informed me he was of the opinion that my car was getting to be very old and I should consider replacing it. I could not believe he was saying this. I told him 'that car runs just fine' and asked him why in hell he would say such a thing to me. Then he really made me mad. He had the nerve to say 'it's just getting to be too old, and that's the long and short of it.'

"Look I told him, I'm older than that car is and are you ready to tell me you think I should be thrown away?"

"What did he say to that?"

"Let me tell you, boy. That lousy pup had nothing left to say. He just turned around and walked down the sidewalk."

Chris did buy a cake of Lifebuoy soap. Then he worked on his courage. The next time Emil came in, Chris timed his play. When a car pulled up to a pump he handed Emil the soap as he skipped out the door. He took a good amount of time pumping the gas, checking oil, cleaning the windshield and collecting the money. That finished, he went back into the station while giving Emil a quick glance.

Emil looked at him steadily. "Thank you, Chris." Emil left for home.

He visited again the next day. The man was in good condition and as friendly as ever. Chris was relieved that there were no apparent hard feelings and felt happy for both of them. *Thank you, Dicke Beck.*

Emil didn't show up again for a week or so. Then he came in early in the work day, again clean and fairly sober. Right after he arrived, a car entered the lot and pulled up to the gas pumps. Chris approached the car admiringly. It was a 1948 Studebaker Starlight Coupe, a vision in glass-work with the rear windows curved around to the sides. The color was yellow. The car glowed in the afternoon sun.

The driver, a lovely young woman, fashionably dressed—skirt ending below her knees, emulating the "New Look"—left the car and walked toward the building. She called,

"Fill her, please," over her shoulder as she passed Chris. He watched as she walked away.

Chris filled the tank with Ethyl gas, then checked the oil and washed the windshield lovingly. The driver had not returned to the car so Chris went into the station to collect.

Emil was alone in the office. *She must be in the restroom*. As Chris started to say something to Emil, a commotion began inside the restroom.

"She's kicking the door." Emil looked puzzled, concerned.

"She might be locked in," Chris said.

Before he could act on the thought, a loud scream came from the restroom. Both men started simultaneously for the door. Emil arrived first. He yanked at the knob. The door rattled against the inside hook. Emil snapped his forearm violently, the hook gave way and the door swung open.

"Quick, Chris, help me." Chris moved to Emil's side. The young woman lay on the floor, quivering violently.

"We must get her out of there. Be careful with her, Emil ordered.

Chris obeyed. They laid her gently on the floor in the office.

She appeared to be unconscious. Her eyelids fluttered, and when they were open her eyes were rolled back. Emil moved her onto her side...gestured to Chris to hand him some clean shop towels. He placed them between her head and the floor. Despite the heat of the day she was wearing a blouse buttoned to the neck. Emil unbuttoned the top button.

"We need an ambulance, Chris...call the County Hospital." Emil's command was quiet and firm.

Chris grabbed the phone, got the operator and placed the call. "God knows how long this will take," he said. Emil did not respond.

The woman was regaining consciousness. She seemed confused. Her head turned side to side, her eyes darted left to right. Her lips moved, but she was unable to form words.

Emil took her hand. She didn't notice. He pinched the skin of her forearm without getting a reaction. He seemed to expect that and nodded his head. "Numbness," he muttered to himself.

"I'll get her some water." Chris headed for the water cooler.

Emil stopped him. "No, nothing by mouth." He followed with, "This is a seizure." He turned back to the woman.

She managed a few words without stringing them together into a sentence. Then, after a short while, she reached with her free hand to her forehead. "My head, oh my head, it hurts so much."

Emil told Chris, "Fold a clean shop towel, soak it with cool water and give it to me."

Chris did and Emil laid it on the woman's forehead. It seemed to give her some relief.

Where the hell is that damn ambulance?—Chris was anxious.

She lay there for quite a while. A siren in the east grew louder as the ambulance approached along the Rock Road. Sidmon and Son had been dispatched by the County Hospital.

The woman wanted to get up. Emil said, "Do not try to restrain her, but be careful to steady her so that she does not fall."

At that moment, the ambulance arrived. The driver and an attendant hurried into the station. While the attendant helped the patient to the ambulance, the driver conferred for a few minutes with Emil.

"We'll let her rest in the ambulance for a little while longer. If she shows no signs of beginning another seizure she'll be okay to drive herself home. You did a fine job for her, sir." he told Emil.

They drove the ambulance to the far end of the parking lot and stayed there for maybe 20 minutes. Chris drove her car from the pumps over to the side of the ambulance. Walking back into the station he smiled sincerely at Emil. "You sure as hell did do a fine job, sir." Emil did not answer him. He stood looking into the distance, shook his head. "She'll be all right now." Emil left.

Chris turned his attention to a car at the gas pumps. When he looked again toward the far side of the parking lot, the car and the ambulance were gone.

The next morning Chris called Earl, the boss, told him what had happened. The legend of how Emil "saved the life" of the woman with epilepsy circulated quickly in the neighborhood.

A reporter from the *Wellston Journal* came to interview Chris about the incident. Chris saw no reason not to give the paper most of the details that he knew about Emil. The reporter was impressed and the next edition carried the story almost verbatim.

An organization in Wellston—similar to the Salvation Army—thought it would be appropriate to acknowledge Emil's actions. They invited him to speak before their group, to tell everyone his inspiring story. They wanted him to know that people were ready to accept him, that he had a future in America.

Emil was surprised and touched...and he accepted. He wrote a short speech which he showed to Chris. He said he was nervous, that he used to speak publicly in the old country but never here. However, he said he was ready.

The Log Cabin Gas Station

For several days before the scheduled talk Chris noticed a continued improvement in Emil's grooming. There was no indication of any drinking. On the other hand, the closer the time for Emil to speak, the more nervous he became. Noticing this, Chris tried to reassure him he would be among friends, that there was no need for him to worry.

On the night of the talk a surprisingly large crowd assembled in the Hall. The group leader made a short introductory talk, the curtains were parted slightly. Emil stepped through, stopped a few steps short of the podium, appeared to be a little unsure of himself. He looked around the room, began to speak, paused, tried again. Still short of the podium, and with a silly grin, he spoke a long sentence in German: *"Ich bin traurig, zu sagen, dass ich nervös und mehr als eine getrunkene Spitze bin."*

He started again to walk in the direction of the podium. He stopped. His knees slowly weakened. The grin faded, became quizzical, worried, frightened—finally, blank. He could not finish. He was on the floor.

Several concerned folks rushed from the audience to help him. Smelling salts appeared from more than one purse.

"What did he say—just before he fell?" The question seemed to come from everywhere. A small woman—a bun of gray hair piled atop her head—supplied the answer: "He said in German, 'I am sorry to say I am nervous, and more than a bit drunk.'"

Emil did not return to the Log Cabin for almost a week. When he did, he was quite drunk and stunk as bad as he ever had.

LUCIUS

*Lucius,
through the kindness of an old friend,
is given a new life.*

LUCIUS

"Lucius...get out of that hole and get up here now. Do...you...hear…me?"

Cora Lee's call—aimed at the open cellar door—was met by a prolonged wet cough. She waited a few seconds and yelled down the steps...louder and more imperative this time. Another, shorter cough, and a black face appeared from the darkness below.

Cora stared down, waited, then issued an ultimatum: "Get up here or I'll come down there and get you."

Lucius climbed the stairs to the sidewalk, blinked at the bright sunshine. About a foot taller than the woman, he looked down to ask, "Cora Lee, why are you yelling at me?"

"Because I think you need to get some sun light and warm on that cough of yours.

You *know* that's not good for you, down there all the time."

"Well, Ma'am, you *know* that's where I live. I come up here when I have something to do up here. You got something for me to do?"

"I just told you what I want you to do—get some fresh air and sunshine. Walk up and down the sidewalk for a while."

"Sure...and I get caught doing that, and who's going to feed me...you? I got to keep this job."

Cora was not going to be dissuaded. "All right then. Go back down there, fetch a broom and get right back up here. Sweep up around here."

"Around here" was the sidewalk along the driveway that ran between the back of the apartment building and the row of garages to the rear. Cora Lee London was the senior member of the hired help in the complex. The combination of her gender and seniority placed her in a command position. But more than that, Lucius knew her to be a good person and a friend.

And he did have to admit to himself that his chronic cough should not be taken lightly. He had that cough for almost as long as he could remember.

Born and raised in the rice-growing country of northwestern Mississippi, the cold wetness of his job—if it did not bring about his condition—certainly did nothing beneficial for it. Realizing that fact, Lucius left the farm and made his way to find other work in the big city of Memphis.

It took him just two days of walking to get into the town. The route he took, with no detailed plan or destination aforethought, brought him into the southeast section of the Memphis suburbs. He walked past The Fairgrounds and, not much later, found himself gazing across a large boulevard at a magnificent park. The street signs told him he was at the intersection of Poplar Boulevard and Cooper Street.

He paused to thank the Lord for getting him to Memphis. Now he needed to find work. He decided to turn left on Poplar. He reasoned that this large street would be connected with a business or industrial area, and knowing the Mississippi River bounded the city on the west the logical direction to head would be west.

He began to walk. In the first block on his side of Poplar, across from the park he found himself passing two large handsome apartment houses. The buildings—each two-story brick—were set a good distance back from the street. Their spacious grass lawns were fringed with well-trimmed shrubbery. He noticed a man—a white man—with a rake, near the building, clearing debris from under a large magnolia tree. Nearer to him was another yard man pushing a lawn mower. This fellow gave Lucius a friendly wave as he worked his mower closer to the sidewalk.

During the days on the road, Lucius had become aware of a remission of his cough. He was feeling better in a sunny, drier atmosphere and finding it easier to be sociable. Now he was happy of a chance to chat after several days of being alone.

Lucius returned the greeting. "Afternoon, friend. You sure do have a pretty place to work."

The yard man halted to reply. "Yes, indeed. There's a lot worse jobs than this."

Lucius said, smiling, "I think I need to go find me one."

"You think you can handle a rake?" He pointed with his chin in the direction of the man working near the magnolia tree.

"Well, of course I can. Done enough of it on the farm to learn how."

"If you're looking for work you need to go talk to that man. He's the boss here. He's working that rake because the last man quit his job and Boss hasn't found no one to replace him."

He swung his mower in the opposite direction and headed back toward the building.

Lucius went straight to the Boss, applied for and got the job. "Yes, sir" was the only reasonable response. He learned soon enough

The Log Cabin Gas Station

that the job benefits included a free room—albeit in the basement of the building—and that he had no choice in the matter. He would be expected to live there for seven nights and six days each week so as to be available to the management for any maintenance and handyman help they might require.

The basement room was cool, dark (only one small electric light bulb) and damp. The electric light was a bonus. Lucius was a good reader—best in the grade school in Mississippi—and read at every opportunity. He became a regular subscriber to the *Press-Scimitar* and *Commercial-Appeal*. Daily, he'd glean the Memphis newspapers from the trash baskets in the apartments. He followed the local news and, after Pearl Harbor, the war-news closely. Lucius had a bright analytical mind and he used it well. He noticed, with a feeling of relief, that he'd passed the age limit for the draft a year earlier.

But, before long, his cough returned.

Sundays were his days off. During his early weeks and months in Memphis, Lucius spent his Sundays walking, learning what he could about his new hometown. From childhood he had established "his place" in the white man's world. He filed the rules with the other social mores one observes and learns. He discovered an area on the south side of downtown where folks were compatible, where he could buy and enjoy a Sunday dinner. Before long he had been invited to Sunday service at a church in the vicinity and had met and made a number of friends. One friend, Willie, owned and operated a small café. There Willie produced "the finest barbecue ribs that could be found anywhere."

Later on, Lucius had been offered the opportunity to earn his Sunday dinner by helping Willie at the business. He learned for himself how fine barbecue ribs were prepared.

The fresh air and exercise of walking to Wilson Street and back home each Sunday tended to counter the effects of basement accommodations. By and large his chronic cough stayed under control.

Cora walked and talked alongside him as he swept the concrete sidewalk. She was not busy this afternoon. She came to work after the Rogers' had finished breakfast and completed sweeping and dusting the second-floor apartment before lunch. The cuckoo clock announced noon from the dining room wall. She then prepared scrambled eggs, with a side dish of sliced, fried summer squash for Ms Viola and the boy. Mr. Rogers worked at the office and had lunch downtown.

Cora cleaned up the dishes in the kitchen, and then ate the sack lunch she'd brought from home. She waited around in the vicinity of the apartment in case she was needed, but in general the afternoons were hers. Today, Cora was determined to continue her sermon on Lucius living in "that hole."

"Cora Lee, you understand I need this job, and that I live where I live so I can keep this job. I don't have a choice. I don't know anywhere else in Memphis to find a job I can do."

The woman was quiet for a while, then she said, "Lucius, St. Louis is a much bigger city. It has good weather. Maybe you could find a job there."

"Cora...are you crazy? Everybody knows St. Louis is the most segregated city in the south."

"I hear that too. They *are* strict there, but they are more practical. They don't make trouble just for the fun of it. None of this 'get off my sidewalk' stuff. And, they don't do 'back of the bus' stuff."

"How do you know that, Cora?"

"I'll tell you what I learned from the boy, the nephew of my family," referring to the Rogers family she worked for, upstairs. "One time I took the boy uptown from here on the bus. I got on and went to the back. I turn around to sit and he was getting ready to sit down beside me. The driver never noticed, but everybody on the bus with us did. I told him to get himself up to a seat in the front. He doesn't know what I'm talking about. I told him, 'Don't ask me, just do it.' I told him I'd explain later. I did and that's when I learned how they do it in St. Louis.

"Another thing...they seem to be more respectful of folks. One time, when that child was younger, he came down to stay and he was getting out of hand. I had to tell him about it. I had to tell him he should be more respectful. I could see him thinking about what I said, looking sorrowful. He looked straight at me and said, 'Cora, I apologize.'

"You see what I'm saying?"

Then Cora decided to lighten up. She showed Lucius a warm, friendly smile. "Honey, I see one thing good about that cave you live in—it sure does keep your skin from getting black."

He wagged his head, smiling. "Ah, Cora, you see...there's something good about everything."

Cora felt good about that. It was good to see her friend smile. "You know, Lucius, when I was a child my mother always told me to stay out of the sun, 'It will make you black.' She told me more than once. I should have listened."

She thought a little bit, smiled again. "I just made things worse. When I got a little older she would say, 'Don't you never drink your coffee black—it'll make you black'. I did it anyway...and just look."

The Log Cabin Gas Station

Lucius began to laugh at her silliness. Suddenly the effort brought on a spell of hard and long, deep coughing.

Cora put an arm around his shoulders. "All right, that's enough. I hate to think of losing you to St. Louis but I love you as a friend too much to see you not taking care of yourself. Now get yourself to St. Louis, and pray all the way that you'll find a job where you can live healthy. And when the Lord has answered your prayer—as you and I both know He will—you send me a letter and tell me how you are doing better."

Cora took a piece of paper from her pocket, then a pencil. She licked the tip of the pencil, wrote her address on Wilson Street, and handed it to him. She gave him a long stern look, and turning away walked to the back stair-well and up to the second floor apartment.

Lucius listened intently. He remained on the sidewalk, quiet and thoughtful. He had never considered leaving. But now, suddenly, it took an effort to go back downstairs. Early the next morning he emerged, carrying a tote sack with all his belongings. The sack was plenty light enough to carry anywhere.

Lucius stopped by the Superintendent's office to tell him he was leaving and goodbye. Although he could afford to take the bus uptown, he wanted to walk, to say goodbye to Memphis. It had treated him well.

Near the west end of Poplar he turned off, went by the barbecue stand. There Lucius related Cora Lee's sermon in detail. Willie knew Mrs. London well—from church, and as a good customer. "Lucius, she's a good woman and your friend. You do what she told you," he instructed. "And we're going to start your prayin' right now!"

The long-time friends hugged each other. Lucius started out the door, aiming to cut through Confederate Park toward the bridge.

Came a sudden yell from inside: "Hey...hold up there Lucius...come back in here."

Lucius turned, went back inside, looked at Willie and said nothing.

"I just now remembered. Old Man Weismann'll be bringing in a delivery in about an hour. He'll be going to West Memphis next, to the 'Coffee Pot'. He'll give you a ride to there. Get you across the bridge and to the Frisco tracks.

"Sit down here and have some breakfast with me until he gets here."

Two hours later, Lucius joined the SLSF right-of-way where the tracks bent north for St. Louis. The afternoon sun—now in mid-autumn—felt good on his back and promised a clear, pleasant day. The track bed was relatively smooth, the grade, flat and the road straighter than the highway. Lucius was not interested in speed—he figured he'd get there when he got there—but he was on the lookout for weather conditions and the potential need for shelter. If he saw fruit or berries he'd pick and eat some along the way. He had money to spend for food but he preferred to stay away from towns if possible. After all, he was a stranger in a strange land. He passed a couple of pecan trees and found the ground beneath them littered with fallen nuts. He stuffed his pockets.

Lucius spent the first night under a railroad bridge that crossed a small creek. In the morning he found himself very near the town of Jericho. He bypassed the town without incident. Folks seemed to have enough to do of their own, without taking notice of a stranger.

Watching the sky in the early afternoon, the signs pointed to rain later in the day. Lucius decided to desert the railroad track for the highway. He couldn't count on finding another bridge at the right time and he did not relish the idea of a fast-rising creek chasing him out into a thunderstorm.

Haystacks were plentiful along the road, so he kept one eye on them and one eye on the sky. Shortly after sundown the rains came, and they came in buckets. Lucius had a plan, and he executed it. He spotted a field and made a beeline for a tall, thick haystack. After a warm, dry night he hit the road as the night sky was just showing dawn.

Hal D. Simpkin

The rain had been substantial and the shoulders of the roads were muddy. Watching for an opportunity to gain an open, level, and more or less dry area, he spotted some strange activity in a nearby pasture. He stopped for a better look.

A barbed wire fence ran parallel to the highway. A couple of hundred feet on the other side of the fence there appeared to be a very old man driving a bony mule. Lucius stared through the dim light of early dawn.

The driver saw Lucius looking at him and called out loudly. "Come over here boy. I need help. Please." The anxiety in his voice was unmistakable.

Lucius was used to being called "boy". He never cared for it, but he was philosophical about it—particularly if it was only a figure of speech and he detected no malice in the tag. He climbed hastily but carefully through the barbed wire, and slopped across the rain-soaked field toward the old man. When he finally got close enough, Lucius saw the extent of the problem. Both the spindly man and the pitiful mule were mired in mud.

"Oh my Lord, Grandfather. What's happened here?"

"That darn fool mule was stuck already when I looked for him this morning. It was just getting lighty. When I came out to help him I got stuck in the same mess he's in. I sure hope you can get us out."

The Log Cabin Gas Station

"Well, sir, I'm going to work on you first. I got to get you out of here. When I do, we'll both see what we can do about your mule." Then he added, "Let me look around for something to work with. I'll be right back for you."

There was a stand of old trees about 100 yards farther into the field. Dropping his tote sack, Lucius made his way toward the trees—carefully, so as not to get himself trapped in the mire. The gray clay-dirt sucked at his shoes. Every step required prodigious effort to free his feet for the next step. Finally, he reached the trees—winded and tired. Resting momentarily, he looked around and found what he had hoped for. A fallen limb—about four inches in diameter and seven or eight feet long—was an answer to prayer. Lucius picked it up and started back. The weight of the tree limb increased the grip the muck had on his legs, slowing his progress toward the stranded man and his mule. *I can't take too long. Got to get him out before that sun gets up and bakes us all into this pasture. Lord, set us free!*

He laid the tree limb on the ground about two feet behind the old man's heels, parallel with the man's shoulders. Then Lucius sat down in the mud, behind the log. He bent his knees and put his shoes up against the tree limb. Then he straightened his knees slowly, forcing the limb down into the mud. The wide surface area of the wood added enough resistance to keep the limb from sinking below the surface. Lucius reached forward, grabbed the man under his armpits and straightened his knees. *I hope I don't break him in two*.

The clay seemed to fight to hold the old fellow. Lucius glanced anxiously at the rising sun and gave a desperate, powerful tug. The old man was free!

The mule was not so fortunate. The tired old creature had succumbed to fright and the strain of his own struggle with the mire.

The man looked at his mule and then at Lucius. "It is a gift from God."

Lucius studied the man's face. At first he thought the old fellow did not realize that his critter was gone.

Then the old man explained. "The poor thing was so tired and wore out that I knew I was going to have to put him down. Just couldn't get around to doing it. I didn't have the heart. I saw him out here this morning and felt something was wrong. Guess he wanted to take care of it himself."

Lucius picked up his tote sack and turned toward the fence.

"Come back here boy. You can't leave yet. Let's sit under that tree, let me catch my wind and I'll fix us some breakfast."

Lucius stopped on the front porch, took off his muddy shoes, left them there. He pulled his clean pair of pants from his sack. Removed his muddy pants and shook off what he could from the seat and cuffs. Turned them inside out and stowed them in the tote sack.

Breakfast was over and Lucius was helping with the dishes when they heard the roar of a powerful engine in the driveway behind the kitchen. The man opened the door and looked out. "Well, what do you know...it's my nephew, Harold. I wonder what he's up to."

He turned to the door and called, "Come on in here, young man. What brings you here today?"

The young man turned out to be in his middle 40s and big enough to make two each of both his uncle and Lucius. "Aw, I just stopped by for a cup of coffee. I've got to take that load all the way to St. Louis today and I'm going to need all the caffeine I can get."

The uncle set another cup on the table and filled it from the pot that he and Lucius had been working on. He introduced his nephew to Lucius and told him the whole story of the morning, from the time Lucius climbed through the barbed wire fence until he found the old mule dead.

"That's quite a story, Lucius. It sure looks like my uncle was a lucky man that you came by. How did you happen to be along there, anyway?"

"Well, sir," Lucius began, "I'm walking my way to the same destination as yours. Fortunately—at my speed—I don't need to get there today."

Harold stroked his chin, thought silently for several seconds, looked up at Lucius. "Well, would you like to?" Lucius looked at him dumbfounded—said nothing.

"I'll make you a deal, Lucius, if you want. I'll drive that rig, and you keep me awake all the way. I'll get you to St. Louis—at least just outside it. Alright?"

"Yes, sir, it surely is." Lucius smiled at the old man. "Another gift from the Lord today."

The old man beamed, nodded his head, silently.

"Here you are Lucius. As promised. Corner of Lindbergh and St. Charles Rock Road." Harold pointed right. "That way is St. Louis. You're on the edge of it now. I have to go the other direction, to get this load to St. Charles City—just across the river. Good luck to you, and many thanks for all the good conversation. You kept me awake the whole entire trip."

He extended his hand, Lucius grasped it and they shook. Lucius opened the door, stepped out, closed it and waved. The truck engine roared as Harold turned his rig left and headed out the Rock Road for St. Charles.

Lucius began to walk eastward on the Rock Road, in the direction of his new hometown. The mid-afternoon sun felt good on his back. *I wonder how this road got its name.*

The Log Cabin Gas Station

Doesn't seem to be rocky to me. Seems like a mess of hard clay, busted up concrete and bumps. Oh well, as long as it gets there.

He'd put in about a half mile and had seen nothing at all that resembled a big city— or a city of any size. Then the car pulled up alongside him. *Oh man...what's this? Police man, maybe? Black man don't need to be walking along this road without a reason?*

Lucius turned his head slowly, looked over carefully at the car and driver. Both front windows were rolled down. A white face smiled and called to him. "I'm going as far as Wellston. Can you use a ride?"

"Well, yes sir, if it's all right with you."

"Well, of course it's all right with me. Would I have stopped if it wasn't?"

"Yes, sir, er, no, sir. I imagine you wouldn't have."

The driver smiled, leaned over and opened the passenger side door. "Get in." Lucius did, noticing the car to be a brown 1936 Plymouth.

The driver kept up a lively conversation and soon learned that Lucius was fresh in town from Memphis. "An old friend of mine comes from Memphis. Maybe you've heard of him... W. C. Handy. Have you?"

"Well, yes, of course, sir. The man writes the Blues. Lots of people know about him. He's your friend? How did you come to know him—if I could ask?"

"I grew up with his brother, Charley."

"How…how could that be?"

"Charley lived and worked on my father's farm. We worked on the farm together."

The car stopped at the corner of Lucas and Hunt Road. "I have to turn left here. I'll let you out. You have just a short walk straight ahead and you'll be in Wellston. Wellston is a part of St. Louis. It's been a pleasure meeting you, and good luck to you, sir."

Lucius was still making his thanks when the driver smiled, waved, and pulled around the corner.

The Lord was not through with Lucius this day. Lucius looked across the intersection, saw a clean white frame building sitting among a grove of trees. It looked to be a roadhouse.

A sign above the door identified the "CORNER GROVE INN." A smaller sign on the door read—"HELP WANTED."

Not even breathing, Lucius hurried diagonally across the intersection. Climbed the steps. Opened the door. Hesitated, then went in.

The large man behind the bar was the only person in the room, not unusual in mid-afternoon. He saw Lucius standing there, looked at him quizzically, and then—with a more understanding expression—"Oh, are you here about the help-wanted sign?"

Lucius assured him that he was indeed looking for work. He held his head up—looked straight into the older man's eyes.

When the man behind the bar, who identified himself as Logan, told Lucius the jobs he needed done—janitor and handyman—Lucius told him of his years of experience at the apartment building.

Logan was happy to realize his job was filled. He named the pay. Would that be okay?

Lucius gulped, swallowed, "Oh, yes, sir. That will be just fine." *It will be better than fine!*

He had one more thing to add. "Logan, (he'd already been told emphatically to call the boss by his first name), I noticed you have a barbecue pit on the side of the building. I've been cooking for years at the best rib house in Memphis."

Logan sucked in a little air and said: "Lucius, you just got yourself a raise. Oh, and if you don't have a place to live, I've got a little place around back you can use if you want."

"Well, that would be fine. Is it in the basement?"

"Hell no, it's not in the basement. There's a little frame building behind this one. I hope you can use it. It would be good to have you available."

GYPSIES

*Chris is given an object lesson
in thoughtfulness.*

GYPSIES

  Lucius was mad—damn mad. And if someone had asked him why he would have been happy to tell them why he felt he was justified. And that someone might have said that Lucius had a case. The foreign bastards had encroached upon his territory and when he appealed to Logan for permission to run them off, permission was denied.
  "Lucius, they are customers, or at least they probably will be as soon as they are ready to come in. So, what you say we leave them alone and treat them with respect?"
  "Yeah, but Logan, I've got to get the barbecue started." Lucius was as respectful as anyone, but right now he had to deal with a priority decision. After due thought, the people

who had parked that contraption up against his barbecue grill were going to come in second.

"Tell you what, Lucius." Logan was willing to spend a little time helping Lucius solve his problem. "Why don't you walk out there and ask them if there is something you can get for them. Maybe they'll tell you they want some barbecue; then you can tell them you'd be happy to make some but they need to let you get to your grill."

The contraption in question looked to be a homebrew motor home, built upon a medium-sized truck chassis. It was not ugly but it was homely. And its presence there was getting to be a concern to Logan himself. The motor home had pulled up to the east side of the Corner Grove Inn building—close alongside the concrete block barbecue grill. Lucius, the janitor and handyman at the Inn, was trying hard to get started on his favorite job. Twice a week on a floating schedule Lucius donned a clean apron and produced the finest barbecue that could be found along that part of St. Charles Rock Road. And today was to have been one of those days.

"Dammit, Logan, if I could squeeze in between the pit and that damn truck and start the fire and smoke going, they'd damn sure back away."

"Aw…cool down, my man. Let me go out and have a talk with them. See what they are looking for and see how you and I can help them. Okay?"

Lucius thought that he'd better say nothing, so that's what he said. Logan came out from behind the bar, removed his apron and told Lucius to watch the place while he went out to talk to the driver. The barroom was empty at the time so Lucius had nothing to watch, and figured he could do that. "Okay, Logan."

Well, Lucius is right about one thing. That guy behind the wheel does look like some kind of foreigner.

As Logan neared the driver's door the driver opened it, got out, smiled and raised his right hand in greeting. "Good afternoon, sir. You have a nice shady spot here." And it was true. The stand of large box elder trees that gave the Inn its name did provide fine shade on a hot sunny afternoon.

"Well, sir," Logan returned the amenities, "I thank you for saying so, but now I need to ask you to move your vehicle away from the barbecue pit. My man is about to come out here and go to work on some barbecue."

The little dark man, whom Logan was addressing, looked surprised and seemed embarrassed. "Oh, I didn't notice, I am sorry, I did not realize." To Logan, the man seemed overly apologetic, at least a little so. He got back into his truck and began the process of moving and re-parking the vehicle about 15 feet away from the grill, still parallel to the east side of the building.

The driver opened his window, put his head partially out of it, smiled and waited for approval.

"That's fine, thank you," said Logan. "Now if you'd like to come in I'll be happy to serve you."

"No, that's all right, we'll be in later." The driver closed the window and disappeared from view.

Logan thought that to be a little odd. He shook his head once, turned and walked around to the front of the building, back up the stairs and into the barroom.

It was a little cooler that day...the day the motor home pulled in alongside the Corner Grove Inn. From the Log Cabin Gas Station, next door, Chris Christopher had seen it arrive and then watched for quite a few minutes as nothing further happened. For Chris to think of the contrivance as a motor home was really a kindness. It was more of a large box—or small house—somehow affixed to the bed of a flatbed truck.

As hot as the day had become there was still no apparent activity around the "house" until later in the afternoon. Then, one by one, occupants began to step out of the driver's side door of the truck. First an older man, small and dark of skin, then a linebacker-sized man in his early 20s, followed immediately by another who could have been his twin brother. These two were not nearly as dark as the first.

Another 20 minutes elapsed. The right-side truck door opened. An attractive olive-skinned woman stepped down. She appeared to be somewhere in age between the older man and the two younger. She walked around to the back of the vehicle and, using her knuckles, rapped on the back wall.
A door swung open. From somewhere inside, a stepladder was handed down and hooked at the top to the truck bed. A young girl backed down the ladder.
At this point, Chris began to pay more attention. He thought, "She's beautiful." She looked up and saw him looking at her. She smiled, then turned her head and looked down. Chris saw the older woman looking steadily at him and turned away. At that moment a car pulled into the station driveway and Chris moved to take care of business.

Soon after, Earl, the general manager of the company's chain of gas stations, called to tell Chris that the night man was sick. Would Chris be able to pull two shifts tonight? Chris was happy. He would be paid at a bonus rate for the extra hours. Later in the evening, business would slow to almost nothing and he could catch some sleep. The pneumatic bell would wake him if a car did drive in. All around, this was a good deal. *After all, I'm here for the money.* He loved it. Pile up the dollars. He'd need it, come September.

Chris hustled over to the Corner Grove Inn to get a couple of sandwiches for his supper. The new group from the motor home was at a table in the far back corner. Chris went to the bar to place his order with Logan. Logan turned to Lucius who had heard Chris' order. Lucius went to work on it.
"Hey, Logan, who are those people?"
"Oh, just a family of Gypsies. They're parking next door for a couple of days."
"Gypsies, huh? What are they doing around here?"
"Oh, you know...whatever Gypsies always do. They asked me if I wanted them to provide some entertainment for the customers—no charge to me. The mama tells fortunes, the kids play a little music, the girl dances. They pass the hat and collect what they can. I told them, `Sure, go ahead. It's good for business.'"

Logan had already informed Lucius that the family were Gypsies and told him to quit thinking of them as foreigners. "They're

Americans and that makes them as good as you or me." Lucius held his tongue.

    Chris did not hear her approach. He had been sitting at the desk for 20 or 30 minutes, reading and keeping an eye on the driveway. So far, no cars had interfered with his reading. He saw—or sensed—the movement in the door to his right, glanced up and saw the Gypsy girl from next door. If his heart missed a beat he was not aware of it. For an instant he was not aware of anything that he would have been able to define—his reflexes had him totally, completely aware of her. He swallowed, gasped, and came up smiling. He stood there, entranced. She returned the smile for just a second and then looked into his eyes with a quiet, steady gaze.

    She was a small, trim young woman—more young woman than girl. Her complexion was deeply pigmented, olive, but with a tinge of tawny glow. Her eyes were black and piercing, with an indescribable luster. She had blue-black hair, worn straight and at shoulder length. Her features were regular—mouth not small, lips lovely in form, nose straight with a slight hook. She had small flat ears, pretty hands and small feet. To Chris, she was a vision of loveliness.

    "Hello, I am Violça. What is your name?"

    "Did you say your name is Viola? Er...I'm Chris."

"No, my name is Violça. I am happy to meet you, Chris."

He took a moment to think about her name, then... "Violça, that's pretty. I have never heard it before."

"It means a certain flower—a violet flower. It is my flower."

Chris liked that. It gave him a happy feeling to think about it, to realize that she had shared that knowledge with him. He smiled warmly at her without saying anything. He saw a quiet confidence about her. She was wholly different from any girl he knew.

Violça noticed the St. Christopher medal that Chris wore on a neck chain above his collar. She lifted it gently, studied it, released it. "Good."

Now, with a faint smile and a tilt of her head, she turned away from him and slowly surveyed the office. She strolled from object to object, pausing to evaluate each and every thing that caught her eye. There was the soda cooler, the closed door to the restroom, the bulk-oil tanks along the back wall, the shelves with quart cans of several brands of motor oil. As she strolled, looking, Chris heard her softly humming an odd tune—her voice reminiscent of the mellow tone of a violin. At the corner she looked through the open door of the back storage room, turned on a heel and returned to the soda cooler.

"I came for a soda pop for my mother."

The Log Cabin Gas Station

Chris was quick to notice that—*Logan sells sodas.* "Sure, would she like a Pepsi-Cola? Or..."

"I think she'd rather have a fruit flavor." Her pronunciation of "fruit" was "flute"—the only hint of an accent that Chris had noticed. She handed him a nickel.

"Oh, no, that's all right. I'll be glad to give it to her."

"No, thank you. My mother would not want that, but thank you."

Chris handed her a *Nu-grape*. Her eyes narrowed slightly. She looked deep into his. "I will come back tonight...for you." She gave him a coquette's smile, turned and left in the direction of the motor home. Chris slumped into the desk chair. He needed to gather the thoughts that seemed to be in the air, everywhere around him. He was very happy.

All afternoon his mind was on the coming night. He was young, he was fascinated, he was randy.

The night shift business was slow, as slow as it had ever been. The after-work rush hour ended. Drivers filled up, hurried home for dinner and stayed to listen to the ballgame.

Darkness fell and within 30 minutes Violça returned. She walked into the station office without saying anything. She looked around, smiled at Chris. "Come, lover. Come with me." She gave him her right hand. He stood, his mind blank, and held her small hand tightly. She led him into the storage room. The room, dark except for the light coming from the office, contained nothing other than several stacks of cardboard cartons of oil cans. One tall stack stood behind the open door. A shorter stack was on the floor in front of it. Together they formed a satisfactory chair. Violça sat down on the low stack, leaned back and pulled him to her. She pulled his head down to hers, raised her mouth to his. She kissed him warmly, wetly, and held it for many seconds.

Violça ended the kiss—he wanted another. He reached for her neck and placed his mouth on hers. She turned her head, took his right hand and spread her legs. She drew his hand between them. She wore nothing under her skirt.

Sensations of corn silk and warm olive oil. And yielding flesh. Her aroma filled the room.

She kissed him again. With his left hand, Chris tried to get rid of his uniform pants. The elastic waistband wouldn't cooperate. He would not remove his right hand from that magic place. Frantic now, he struggled without success.

Violça reached around him, placed her hands on the small of his back, slid them downward, stripping his uniform and undershorts to his ankles. She raised her hands to his hips, drew him to her.

It was over in a moment. They clung to each other in the stifling room.

An insistent horn, honking from the driveway, seemed far away...then grew closer as he tried to focus. He pulled away, dragged his clothes into shape hastily. Embarrassed now, he hurried to tend to the gas pump.

Violça tried to slip out of the door and toward the motor home without being noticed. The woman—as she was paying for her gas—saw the girl leave. She watched, smiling winsomely.

The following morning—after a night of tossing, turning, and half-awake dreams—Chris drank the last of the coffee from his thermos. The midnight man had just left for home. Violça walked down from the motor home and into the station, looking radiant. She smiled tenderly. "Good morning, my man.... I have something for you." She handed him a small box. It was without a lid. It contained a pair of gold earrings.

"You will wear these. We will be lovers. I will make the holes in your ears for you."

Aghast, Chris stammered. "No, no, you can't do that." He was having—for all the reasons he may have had for being appalled—

visions of his buddies viewing those things in his ears. He shook his head. "No, uh-uh, no!"

He looked at her face, into her eyes. She was miserable, stricken. Tears were forming. Immediately, he felt terrible—terrible for her, then defensive for himself. *What could she be thinking...what right does she have to think that, to do that?*

His reaction to his own thoughts wasn't good. He lashed out....

"You've been seeing too many movies!" He was thinking of a popular movie, still playing in the first-run theaters. Ray Milland played a GI opposite Marlene Dietrich. Dietrich was in the role of the gypsy, the woman who disguised Milland as a gypsy to save him from Nazi soldiers.

Chris regretted his words before she heard them. It was too late. Displaying amazing control, she fought back tears, removed any sign of emotion from her face, turned her back to him and walked slowly from the station toward her home.

He watched them come. Up close, it was clear; they were indeed twins. Well-made, they were of medium stature, three or four inches below Chris' height. They were full-chested and muscular. Their hair was jet black and straight. Although lighter of skin than Violça, Chris recognized them as the brothers he had seen in the Corner Grove Inn. He stepped back into the office.

They stood outside the open office door. One of them asked, "May we come in?"

Chris sensed that his answer would be irrelevant. "Sure, come in." He stood up.

The twin who had asked permission to enter continued the conversation. "You are Chris, right?" He did not wait for affirmation. "Our sister came home from here this morning. She is sad, very sad. Can you tell us about it?"

Chris shifted his attention from the speaker to the other man, then back. He tried to read their faces, to get an idea of what he was up against. He saw the same placid expression on each face. This was unnerving. There was no clue. An experienced poker player, his feet were on the ground when he confronted confidence, assertiveness, aggressiveness or anxiety. Given one of these reads he knew how to play his hand.

He studied the faces of the two brothers and he saw nothing. They looked at him, waiting for him. Uncertain, he responded...trying to remain calm and earnest in return. He intended to speak calmly but he did not feel totally calm.

He moved into uncharted territory. "I know that when Violça left here, she was not happy. And I know that it was my fault."

His words were met with slight frowns and continued earnest attention. The two brothers moved and reacted identically.

Chris continued, "I want you men to know—although I have not known your sister very long—I have become very fond of her. She is such a sweet, kind young lady. She came here this morning to give me a gift, and I—I am sorry to say—I refused her gift ...badly."

The two brothers were attentive. They wanted to hear more. Beginning only with this morning, he told them, in detail, about the earrings, her offer to pierce his ears and his surprised, thoughtless response to her.

The brothers turned to look at each other, mumbled a brief conversation that Chris couldn't understand, and turned back to him, chuckling.

The heretofore silent twin shook his head, then spoke. "Women! My God, they can be silly. She needs a good bawling out!"

Chris was caught off balance. Sincerely dismayed, he spoke quickly, too loudly. "No, don't hurt her. She didn't do anything wrong. I was not kind. Let me try to make it up to her. Maybe there's something I can get? A necklace...a little radio?" *What made me say radio?*

The brothers were touched. "Sure, that would be nice. But we will still need to explain to her, to teach her about being realistic."

The brothers offered their hands, shook with Chris, smiled and left. Chris felt a wave of relief. That surprising outcome was one he had not dreamed of. Now realizing the ball was back in his court he was eager to take care of his responsibility. He needed to bring all this to a close.

That afternoon, as soon as the evening-shift man arrived, Chris jumped into his car and drove into Wellston. He found a compact table-model radio, covered with blue artificial alligator skin, trimmed with gold bands of some elastic material. He bought it and hurried back to the station. Gift in hand, he hustled across the parking lot and rounded the edge of the grove of trees. The motor home was gone!

Confused, still carrying the radio, Chris climbed the steps, entered the Inn. A couple of men were drinking beer at the front of the bar. Other than them the large room was empty, save for Logan polishing glasses at the far end of the bar. Chris headed straight for Logan.

"Hey, where'd they go?" Logan realized he was asking about the gypsies. The story Chris heard left him disconcerted and empty.

Intentionally or not, the father of the family had paid for something with a phony ten dollar bill. Lucius spotted it, returned it with a comment that precipitated a squabble. The squabble ended with one of the brothers having a superficial knife-slice on his arm and

Hal D. Simpkin

the family packing up and leaving, motivated by Logan's threat to call the law.

Chris had a short beer, a pickled egg, and took his new radio back to the station.

WATCH OUT FOR THE CHEATER

*Chris demonstrates that he can take care of himself
when faced with unethical treatment.*

WATCH OUT FOR THE CHEATER

Log Cabin was a 24-hour gas station. Earl was shorthanded, and that was the good part. Chris Christopher jumped at every opportunity to put in extra hours. This was summer vacation and next semester expenses were not far away. Fatter paychecks built the bank account.

Chris really enjoyed the job—pumping gas, doing minor auto repairs and meeting interesting people. Every car that drove in brought something new and different.

Earl managed the Log Cabin Gas Station and several other "PowerPump" company locations. Chris' willingness to accept erratic shift assignments and additional overtime made life easier for Earl. He appreciated Chris' flexibility and work ethic.

    This evening Chris was completing an eleven-hour workday. He had been called to work midway in the first shift—at about 1:00 p.m. The dayshift man had been called to handle an emergency at home. By midnight—the end of his regular evening shift—Chris was whipped. It had been a busy and frustrating day, one of those days when interruptions occurred just when pump traffic was heaviest and interruptions were as likely-as-not to be interrupted themselves. And it had been a regular August hot one—three hours after dark—thermometer still over 80.
    Chris had seen workdays like this before. He had handled this one as expeditiously as could be expected—the kind of performance that gratified Earl. Nonetheless when midnight, Lew and the end of the evening shift finally arrived, he was a tired puppy—as Uncle Dicke Beck would say.
    Lew saw his evening shift counterpart about to fall asleep. The older man (by eight or nine years) suggested that maybe Chris would like to grab a nap before driving home. Lew—who himself was an experienced member of the station crew and seemed the manifestation of a Good Old Boy—offered to handle the paperwork that went with every shift change.

The Log Cabin Gas Station

A necessary part of the job, tie-in paperwork was still a pain. For the duration of his shift the attendant on duty was responsible for all stock-in-trade on the premises and for all of the cash. Each gasoline pump had a meter that displayed the number of gallons of gas it had dispensed. These numbers were recorded at the beginning and end of each shift. The change in meter readings represented the sales made by the attendant on duty. The attendant was responsible for the money collected from the customers.

At each shift change, outgoing and incoming attendants walked together from pump to pump, recording meter readings. They signed their agreement with the record. Throughout the shift the attendant—after holding out enough cash for making change—would put the paper money into an envelope, sign his name on the envelope and deposit it through a slot in a steel safe buried in the concrete floor. Coins in the belt-hung change-maker were counted, recorded and passed to be hung on the belt of the incoming man.

All sales of canned and bulk-oil, cigarettes and even bottled pop, had to be accounted for. The items were counted piece-by-piece and sales were similarly recorded.

Signed record-sheets were then dropped into the safe, completing the transfer of responsibility. Every morning a messenger in an armored car opened the safe and picked up the contents. Calculations were performed in the downtown office. Any discrepancies were applied to the paychecks of the erring attendants.

Lew's offer to complete the shift-change inventory by himself may have been entirely altruistic. But Chris had accrued business-world experience during several years of part-time jobs. He was not a gullible young man. If he hadn't been so dog-tired, he would never have accepted the offer. But this time was an exception. Without further consideration he muttered his thanks to Lew, dragged himself to the east side of the building where his Model A Ford waited. He curled himself up on the front seat and fell into the deepest of sleep.

A couple of hours later Chris awoke to sounds of Lew pumping gas and joking loudly with the customer. Still groggy, he went into the station, used the restroom and opened a Pepsi. The completed inventory form, already signed by Lew, awaiting Chris' signature, was lying on the desk. Already apprehensive, Chris could do nothing but sign his name. He signed and dropped the form into the safe.

At the end of the week his paycheck arrived with a deduction for "Inventory Shortage" of $8.36, just about a hard day's pay.

Later in his shift when business slowed, Chris tilted back, feet on desk and lit a cigarette. He reviewed what had happened, what he had done to cost himself a day's pay. He knew he had himself to blame. After all, he reasoned, Lew might have made an honest mistake in reading the pumps. With a crowded lot it would be tough enough for two attendants to get it right; Lew had voluntarily taken the burden upon himself.

But, on the other hand, Chris told himself, *I really can't believe that's the explanation. I've never seen a crowded lot at midnight. The pumps were easy enough to read. The inventory form was easy enough to complete. Lew is an experienced attendant and a clerical error at that tie-in is just too much of a coincidence to accept.*

Chris was smarting but he had no proof. He knew there was far more to lose than gain by calling Lew out on what had been done. After all, his own responsibility for that shift was not completed until he participated in the inventory reading and signed off for himself. Actually he was still on duty and had no business being asleep. He decided not to say a word to Lew. He believed he'd been taken; he resolved to even the account in his own way, at the appropriate time.

The following week an opportunity presented itself.

Lew had agreed to work the Friday midnight-to-8:00 a.m. shift, as a favor to a friend. Learning this, Chris arranged for his hours on Thursday to be 4:00 p.m. until midnight. He would be tying-in to Lew. He would then come back in to work, after eight hours rest, to work the Friday day shift. That way, Lew would be handing-off to Chris at 8:00 a.m. on Friday, the following morning.

Thursday night before his shift ended, Chris loosened the knurled knobs above the lids of the bulk-oil containers, thus allowing the threaded dipsticks to extend further into the oil in the tanks. A higher level of oil was then indicated in both tanks. Moving to the restroom he took four cigarette cartons from the storage shelves. He carefully peeled open one carton each of Chesterfield, Camel, Old Gold and Lucky Strikes and removed two packs of cigarettes from each carton.

Using a long wooden dowel he carefully arranged the remaining packs so that—even if casually opened—the cartons would appear to be full. He pushed the flaps of the opened ends against the wall to keep them closed. He then placed the individual packs on the shelf in the office, ready to be sold one pack at a time.

Chris then appropriated a few of Lew's supply of empty quart oil-cans. These he used to replace a number of full cans in the cardboard boxes in the storage room. A casual look into any cardboard box would give the appearance of cartons full of oil. He placed the full cans on the shelves in place of the empty ones that he'd removed.

Now seated at the desk, the business major grinned at the wall. *I've just created a Barmecidal increase in the inventory...of about eight and one-half-bucks.* He leaned back in his chair...smiled, and began a nap.

Chris tied-in the inventory to Lew at midnight and went home to get some rest. Seven and one-half hours later Chris was back at the station, smiling, asking Lew how the night went.

Shortly after the arrival of Chris, well before he and Lew were ready to begin the morning tie-in, a car pulled onto the lot. The driver of that car just happened to be Chris' old friend Bob Gardener.

Bob elected to stop at the West Island pumps. At that location, an attendant who'd be waiting on him would be working in a place from which he could not see into the open door or front window of the station building.

Bob wanted his tires checked, his radiator level checked, his windshield and rear window washed. He asked then for the attendant—who of course was Lew—to please check the rear bumper to see if it might be loose and therefore be the source of a rattle he'd been hearing.

Fortunately for Lew he had no other customers on the lot. Fortunately for Chris, *he* had ample time to tighten the knurled knobs above the oil tanks. That drew up the dipsticks sufficient to indicate a considerably lower measure of oil in each tank.

Then, he quickly gathered 16 packs of cigs from the office shelf and returned them to their cartons. The flap on each carton was deftly sealed with a dab of library paste. The full and empty quart-size oil cans were switched back to their former locations.

Chris could now comfortably sit at the desk and light up a cigarette before Bob's car had been serviced.

Lew, not the swiftest swallow in the barn, frowned a couple of times at the numbers he was seeing in the inventory. He didn't have enough grasp of the problem to contest it.

Chris signed him out, Lew signed Chris in, and the wrong was righted. The necessary adjustment would be credited by the office to Chris' paycheck.

Chris and Lew had worked together for some time with no trouble. Chris had nothing against Lew but then he had nothing for him either.

Lew was a crude, coarse kind of guy—a fatass who sold porno pictures and cheap booklets to customers of like tastes and to

The Log Cabin Gas Station

teenage boys. Chris neither approved nor disapproved. It was not his responsibility to do so.

Some weeks earlier Lew had proudly informed Chris of his discovery of a mechanical flaw in the switch on the center East Island pump. Pumps of that design were equipped with a switch to be pulled by the user to simultaneously apply power to the pump motor and to return to zero. The meter then showed gallons sold and the price. This particular pump had a defect. Instead of returning to zero dollars it would display $0.50.

Gleefully, Lew demonstrated this phenomenon to Chris. The next time a customer pulled his car up to the defective pump, stopped so the dial on the pump was behind his head and out of convenient view, Lew placed the gasoline hose into the tank fill-pipe and pulled the switch on the pump. The dial read $0.50. Lew begin to pump gas, smiling to himself over the pilfered half-dollar now in his pocket.

Also, more than once, Chris watched Lew short-stick a customer who had asked for an oil check.

This fraud consisted of pulling the oil dipstick from the engine block, wiping it clean with the shop towel, then reinserting it, stopping about 1/2 inch shy of all the way. Lew would display the dipstick to the driver, announce that the oil was a quart low and ask if the driver wished to have it refilled. A choice of two brands was available.

If the sale was made, Lew would then walk back into the station office and remove a previously carefully placed, empty quart-size oil can. Then—while still inside the station but within the view of the motorist—he'd make a show of punching the filler spout into the hole in the top of the empty can.

Returning to the car, carefully holding the open end of the filler tool against the palm of his hand "to prevent spilling any oil on the car," Lew finished the show by inserting the nozzle of the filler tool into the oil fill-pipe on the engine block. He'd then pretend to pour—from the empty can—a quart of oil into the oil fill-pipe. Lew would shove the oil dipstick all the way into the block, withdraw it, and present the stick, showing oil all the way to the full line.

"There you are, that got it." He showed the dipstick through the window to the driver. The price of whatever brand the driver had specified was added to the gasoline bill. Money in Lew's pocket.

Although Chris had evened out the cost of playing the sucker to Lew, he still felt the insult. Chris knew he could exact vengeance by reporting Lew's activities. However, he didn't feel right about snitching to the boss. Chris decided that reporting was not in his job description.

A few days later, sitting in the office, bored, Chris was reading the membership book that was given to him when he was required to join the union. He discovered that the contracted hourly rate for his job was three cents per hour more than he was being paid. Still looking for some way to pass the time, he called the phone number given in the Union Member's Book.

The person who took his call listened to his question and told him she didn't know. He asked to speak with someone who did know. She said that would be Mr. Quest and he was not there at the time. "Please have him call me." She agreed to get the message to Mr. Quest.

As promised, a couple of hours later, Mr. Quest returned his call. His explanation for the discrepancy which Chris was questioning was simply, "Regardless of what was printed in the union book, the union had a verbal agreement with *that oil company.*" Chris had never been happy to pay union dues. He worked hard for all the money he was paid and he didn't relish having a significant amount of it deducted by the union. Further, he was a business management major and was already of a very different orientation.

His response to Mr. Quest was, "Okay, now I understand. So I want to make a verbal agreement with you. You don't have to get me the pay rate that you have promised me and I don't have to pay the dues that I promised to you. I will make the necessary arrangements with my company to have them stop paying you from my salary."

Mr. Quest was silent for a moment, then, "I'll come by after a while and explain in person what you need to know." He hung up.

The day was very hot. Business at the pumps was nonexistent. Chris passed the time by reading through the morning *Globe-Democrat* and drinking Pepsi-Cola. He did not have to wait very long for Mr. Quest to make an appearance.

A black 1940 Chevrolet business coupe pulled onto the lot and stopped near the street. A man, probably in his 40s, dressed in business attire, wearing a double-breasted coat and a straw skimmer hat, stepped from the car. He closed the door and waddled briskly toward the station office. The man measured, at an eyeball guess, about five feet in any direction.

Chris rose to meet him and stepped outside onto the chat rock driveway. "You'd be Mr. Quest; am I right?"

The man stopped in front of Chris. He was perspiring profusely. One could guess that he was not pleased by being stopped outside in the sun instead of being invited into the shade of the office building.

Chris cut him no slack. "Please explain your answer to my proposition."

"You need to understand that you don't make offers to me. I'll tell you what you need to know," Quest said with a subdued snarl.

"If that's your answer, it looks like you wasted a trip. I told you on the phone what I plan to do." Chris turned to walk back to the station.

"Hey, you, don't turn your back on me." Quest grabbed Chris by the shoulder, tried to turn him around.

Chris had had enough. He whirled, and using a right hook and doubled fist, returned the push to the shoulder of Quest. "Keep your hands off me."

Quest staggered backward, stumbled and fell upon his copious rear. He roly-polied sideward, pushed himself up with his hands, dusted himself off with his hands, waddled back to get into his car. He delivered *his* message from the open car-window. "This is not going to do you any good." He snapped off two edicts: "You can't work here anymore. You are out of the union." He drove away.

Chris went inside to wash his hands, open another Pepsi, light a cigarette, stub out the cigarette, and step outside to deliver some gasoline to a lonely customer. When he came back in he called Earl. "Earl, it's Chris."

Earl beat him to the punch. "I already heard. Quest is kicking you out of the union."

"He told me I can't work here without being in the union. I guess you'd better get somebody out here right away."

"Let me think about it. I'll get back to you." Chris wondered what that could mean.

Earl did not call back; he drove to the station in less than 20 minutes. He got out of his car, came into the office. "You're to continue working here as always."

"What about 'I have to be a union member'?"

"Not if you are a member of management. You are now the manager of this station."

"Holy cow...really?" Then, "Does this mean I get a raise?"

Earl smiled. "Hell no, get back to what you were doing."

Chris sat down.

Chris thought about the compliment he had received by being named a member of management just to be able to keep him employed there. He now thought it his responsibility to inform his manager of the broken pump and how it was being used to steal from their customers.

Earl, of course, took the revelation seriously. He told Chris to stay away from it—

The Log Cabin Gas Station

he and his management would take it from there.

Relieved to hear that, Chris agreed to back out but he did suggest that Earl have one of his people drive in and stop at the faulty pump.

Earl set it up. When Lew, trying to take advantage of the $0.50 "opportunity" pulled his trick, the friend reported him to Earl. Lew was fired.

Just before Earl tied the can to Lew, he told Lew he was lucky he wasn't going to jail. Lew agreed. He thanked Earl for the break.

Chris heard a few weeks later that Lew had left town, headed east.

PIKE'S POND

Chris is told a haunting story.

The Log Cabin Gas Station

PIKE'S POND

Bob Gardener pulled into the Log Cabin gas station at noontime in midweek. Through the window in the front of the station office he could see Chris Christopher working at the desk. Chris looked up, started to get up and tend to business when he recognized Bob and saw him waving him off. Bob would fill his own tank. Chris went back to his office work.

Bob came into the cabin office to pay for his gas. Chris took his money, then told him to have a Pepsi and a seat. "Let me tell you what happened this morning.

"Dicke Beck drove in very early. I could hear that Model-T exhaust before I saw his car. He pulled into his favorite spot—around the shady side— got out and walked in before I could get up to meet him. I knew something important was on his mind."

Chris' uncle Charley Becker began..."Boy, I'm going to tell you a story just as my brother-in-law John Kleinschmidt told it to me. You know John and I have a number of old fishing buddies. This concerns one—a fellow named Pike— who we all lost touch with years ago.

"Listen to me now. We'll talk about it when I'm finished."

"... and that is final!"

The unpleasant voice of Gladys wafted through the hall from the living room, out the open front door, and penetrated Pike's reverie. Pike rolled his eyes in the direction of heaven and shook his head once, slowly. He activated that portion of his memory that made it possible for him to replay at least the last portion of his wife's homily. He had been developing this memory technique over the years, but since retirement he'd been given much more opportunity to sharpen his ability.

This one was easy—he had heard it so often before. "And if you are sitting there daydreaming about a farm with a pond, forget it, it's not going to happen…and that is final!"

And she was right again. He *was* giving free course to "that inward eye which is the bliss of solitude." A place to go and be alone—just him and some trees and some grass and some fish in a nice-size pond. *That* had been the vision of retirement that kept him going through the working years.

As retirement grew nearer he finally confided in Gladys what he would like to do in the golden years and that's when it began. She was not going to move to a farm, they could not afford to keep their house and buy a retirement place. Nor was he about to rent a place of his dreams just to leave her alone with nothing to do. Not that she ever did anything more than household chores and listen to radio serials. She told him frequently that she felt trapped.

Pike took care of his household responsibilities and he didn't like radio shows much, other than baseball or the news. He liked to read a little but there was no real opportunity for that. If she caught him reading she plucked a new item from her endless list of chores for him to accomplish. Thus went the first year or two of his "freedom".

When he thought about it he realized it was nothing personal. She didn't dislike him. She just didn't care about him. It was that she never wanted to be married—to anyone. She just wanted to get married—to someone. And he was there. He was young and dumb, that was enough.

And she damn-sure didn't want any kids—including his.

He rarely dwelled on it, but when he did he realized that he didn't care much for Gladys. He never discussed this subject with his retired buddies. Once, one old friend allowed as how he had noticed that Pike and Gladys never seemed too close, Pike thought a bit and then admitted, "She *is* a difficult woman."

You'd think she'd be happier if I was off doing something else like fishing—but then a good part of her fun comes from deviling me. Pike shook his head.

Once, a few days before his birthday, out of a clear blue sky Gladys told him he'd be really pleased with what she had in mind for his birthday present. At first he thought little about it, considering her indifference to him. Then one evening his imagination popped open and ran wild. *Something's different. I wonder if she is going to surprise me with a rod and reel and an okay to find a place to fish.*

Then rationality returned. On his birthday she presented him with a paper sack containing a lightweight jacket made of some kind of oil skin or whatever. "You'll ruin your clothes, running outside in the rain."

The years went by. Occasionally he felt the pain of guilt when he would face up to the fact that he did not miss her—not then, not now, not ever. He thought of it this morning—when the sun had not yet risen and the air was chilly and clear. He shifted his position on the bank, poured himself another cup of coffee and began to get his tackle ready and to make plans for the day. He went mentally over his schedule—fish until they slowed up, then pack up and begin the repair job on the front porch.

As a part of the agreement he and the landlady had made when he leased his part of the farm—the part that contained the pond—he would be responsible for necessary maintenance on whatever needed it. Right now a couple of loose boards on the front porch of the farmhouse needed nailing. He enjoyed that kind of work and looked forward to taking care of it.

Then Pike remembered another looming repair job—one that would not be so pleasant—but one that was ever so much more essential. There was a leak in the dam that formed the pond. This problem went right to the soul of his existence—to his fishing spot.

I guess I've been lucky 'til now. The doggone critters were bound to show up sooner or later.

Actually, Pike had never left the muskrat threat to luck. He planned ahead, years earlier, when he leased the property. Cattails, rushes and arrowhead make a pond pleasant to look at and provide great cover for a variety of good fish—but they are a supply of food for muskrats.

Muskrats, if ample food is available, will move into a pond and will burrow a home into an earthen dam. Occasionally the burrow is continued through the other side, causing a leak.

Pike had always confined the growth of aquatic plants to the far, shallow side of the pond, and he limited their growth to a point where the muskrats would look elsewhere for more plentiful food supplies. Perhaps he'd become complacent, or the critters more aggressive. But undoubtedly, he had a muskrat hole in the dam.

Pike examined the outside of the entire dam. To his dismay, the leak was easy enough to find. Water was trickling steadily, not seeping, through the wall.

And much the worst of it was the fact that the leak was several feet from the top of the dam while the normal level of the pond was about 18 inches below the top. He realized that, although muskrat holes were typically made less than a foot below water level, their lodges inside the dam rarely slope significantly downward. Therefore, the location of the exit hole would not be much of a guide to the finding of the entrance hole.

Paddling and probing slowly from his johnboat, he had surveyed—as best he could—the surface of the dam just below the water level. He hadn't found the entrance hole. At times, for reasons not shared by the animals, the critters began their digging much farther below water level. Nevertheless, he needed to find and plug that entrance hole to stop the leak.

Pike studied the problem and pondered the solution. This pond was a typical generations-old Missouri farm pond. It was made by dragging yards of earth—laced with rocks—by means of mule and plow, mule and wagon—animal power and manpower. It was constructed without benefit of any engineering know-how, without any slide rule calculation. Just like every other in existence, it was built with the advice and ingenuity of a neighbor or friend whose own pond was successful and had been built by neighbor and friend, mule and man, years before.

Pike's dam restricted a creek that crossed the farm for centuries before it was a farm. The dam was about 60 feet wide in order to block the valley of the creek. A cross-section of the dam would show sloping sides—each rising at about 60° angles from the stream bed—creating a flat area about five feet wide at the top. The walls were high enough that the dam formed a pond at its upstream side of about nine feet. Because of the lay of the land, water at the far side of the pond was backed up to...say...18 inches.

Pike was an intelligent man and a good planner. Although he had examined the dam on its downstream side and made note of the location of the exit hole, he knew enough about the nature of muskrats to believe that he would be highly unlikely to find the entrance to the tunnel deeper than four or five feet below the surface. Still, the water in the pond was constantly murky, due to the typical muddiness of Missouri pond water.

He paddled his small johnboat back and forth along the upstream side of the dam and convinced himself that he would be unable to see the hole. He knew what he must do to find it. But first, he needed to be prepared with a means of sealing the hole when he did find it.

He needed a flexible, tough, watertight material—big enough to cover a six-inch diameter hole in the underwater surface of the dam. Pike looked around his own home first. In the kitchen he fingered the oilcloth table cover—maybe so, maybe no. The stuff was waterproof but not nearly flexible enough. It would have to conform tightly to the underwater surface of the dam wall around the muskrat hole.

His 1941 Chevy—he had bought it new, just two years ago, right before Gladys died—was parked in the barn. He needed to take it out and drive a little anyway—get some air in the tires. He drove into town and searched through hardware and dry goods stores without success. He got a blue-plate special at the restaurant, aired up the tires and drove home to think about it.

Car safely returned to the barn, he strolled around the little hen yard, walked down to the pond and saw that the water level had dropped noticeably since this morning's fishing. *Time's wasting. I've got to get this thing plugged.*

He shook his head, lowered it, thought, shook it again, walked up the porch stair, past the still-loose floorboards and into the house. He put his hat on the closet shelf. Then he saw it.

The Log Cabin Gas Station

He had never liked that damn jacket Gladys gave him for his birthday. It would do the job! It was late in the day but he was eager to get the job done. He grabbed the jacket and made a beeline for the pond.

He'd rehearsed in his mind the rest of the plan. Wearing his waders, he draped the collar of the opened jacket over his head, letting it hang down his back. Then holding to the roots and plants that grew abundantly above the water line, he let his boots slide down into the water until he was able to hang his full height plus the reach of his upraised arms. He began to work his way around the wall of the dam, feeling for the opening of the muskrat hole with his boot toes.

The search came to a sudden, terrible and final end. Within one second after his boot toe slipped, the weight of his body and his water-soaked clothes tore loose his grip on the roots above the water line. He felt himself slipping deeper into the water, involuntarily opened his mouth and sucked in a deep breath. By this time his head was under the water and he inhaled much of it. The downward slide continued. Face slipping along the muddy wall of the dam, his forehead struck a projecting rock. He was immediately, mercifully unconscious. He never knew any of the rest.

The landlady's daughter and her husband came to a decision on the repair of the dam. It had begun to leak, albeit slowly, after all these years. They decided to cut a temporary spillway and gradually increase its depth until they had lowered the water level sufficiently to uncover the source of the leak.

They suspected the culprit to be a muskrat but recognized that—given the age of this dam—it was possibly a large plant root that had rotted away and permitted some leakage in its way. Anyway, this season was one of plentiful rainfall, the creek was flowing well, and the pond would refill shortly after the repair was made and the temporary spillway was closed off.

The first cut of the spillway at a one-foot depth proved to be insufficient. They had the workmen from town return and cut another foot away. That job was finished late one afternoon. After watching the work being done, the young couple strolled back past the site of the old hen yard—now their little vegetable garden—and up to the porch. "Dammit Janet, help me remember to get that fellow to fix those boards. I can never remember to do that."

On the porch, they looked back over the pond. The conversation turned—as it did now and then—to the story Janet's late mother would tell of the mysterious disappearance of her tenant. "Pike," she said his name was. He just up and left one day.

They shrugged; "Who knows?"

The next morning, they knew. The pair walked down to the pond to check the level after the night with the lowered spillway. There—above the water level—protruded the shoulders, arms, and upper spine of a human skeleton.

What might have been the head of the skeleton was covered by something resembling a piece of plastic sheet. Apparently, the material had been drawn—by the current-flow due to the leak—snugly over the skull, trapping it tight against the surrounding bank.

~~

Dicke Beck wiped at what he was pretending to be a drop of sweat, near the corner of his eye.

"It's a sad story, boy. Pike was a good friend. It's hard to learn that he had to go that way....

But at least we can properly lay him to rest."

BILL

Chris learns that a helping hand can be found in surprising places.

BILL

Friday night. A remarkably cool cold front came through. As usually happened at this time of year, the front spawned a powerful thunderstorm.

The wind knocked down trees—some large—and many dead limbs. Lightning darkened many, many residences and silenced Harry Caray. The cool rain cleaned away the collected dust. It also provided temporary relief from the heat and a fresh supply of humidity.

A little after dawn on Saturday morning, Bill Hunt's outstanding 1932 Buick Coupe came in from the west, pulled across the westbound lane of the Rock Road and up to the West Island pumps. Chris Christopher was always happy when that happened. Hunt's arrival from either direction was always a pleasant event.

A 17-year-old automobile, Bill's could pass for new. It was in cherry condition and in Chris' opinion the choice-model Buick of its year.

Chris left his seat in the office of the Log Cabin Gas Station and strolled out to the pump. As usual, Hunt was already serving himself. It was a generally accepted, friendly thing to do among friends. And Chris and Hunt were becoming pretty good friends, albeit they never met anywhere but here at the station.

"What's the good word, Bill my man?" Chris began the conversation. "Don't tell me you drove through that storm?"

"The hell I didn't, and the word is I'd better fill this thing and get down to the car lot. I could be in danger of losing my room in Columbia."

Bill Hunt had Chris' undivided attention. "What the heck is that all about?"

"Well, it's not really all that ominous, but I *am* way behind on my rent and still no check from the VA. I'm really getting embarrassed about excusing myself to Mrs. Robyn, and I know she is tired of hearing from me. Not that she's ever said anything unpleasant at all about the situation, but I know she could use the money at least as well as the VA can. So I need to get down to South Grand and see if I can sell a car before it's time to get back to Columbia for Monday morning class."

The Log Cabin Gas Station

The two walked into the station office and sat down to continue their talk. Chris was well aware of the GI Bill benefits that were due Bill Hunt. He knew in some detail of Bill's service during the war as a Seabee. He worked on the construction needed in the Philippines to facilitate General MacArthur's return to the islands.

Bill stopped for gas just about every weekend on his way into St. Louis and out again on early Monday mornings. Bill came regularly into town for a weekend of good eating at his parent's house, a chance to see Ruthie, and to make some badly needed money at either of the two South Grand used car lots that were operated by friends of his.

"Mrs. Robyn seems kind of special, to be so patient after all this time. I'd say you're lucky you moved into her house."

Bill could not agree more. "You know, Chris... she goes out of her way to try to help me. When I was leaving this morning she said she was going over to her neighbor's house. She says Sarah has a son who works in Washington, D.C. She's going to see if he could help me get my money from the VA."

He grinned, amused incredulity. "I'll tell you, those little old small town ladies are thoughtful people but, gee, they have no concept of the size of Washington, D.C. Of course, all I said to her was, 'Thank you and don't go to too much trouble.'"

Chris shook his head and chuckled.

Having finished the last of his coffee and with good luck wishes from Chris, Bill departed for Neosho Street in South St. Louis—bound for his parent's house and some breakfast.

Two days later, Bill Hunt drove in bright and early for the Monday morning return trip out Highway 40 to Columbia. He couldn't wait to jump out of his Buick, which he left at the pump, still without a filled tank. He strode to the office with a yard-wide smile on his face. Chris met him at the door.

"Man, you look happy—you must have sold a car."

"I did—but that's not the half of it, my friend, not at all. Let me tell you what did happen.

"Yesterday, right after breakfast, I walked out to the front yard to get the paper for my dad. Then I was heading for the car lot. I tossed the paper onto the front porch and started toward the driveway to get my car. Just then a big, long, black Cadillac sedan pulled up right in front of the house. This is not often seen in the 3700 block of Neosho. I stood there with my face hanging out.

"Both front doors opened. Two men, dressed for big business in suits and ties, got out of the car. I walked across the front of the

The Log Cabin Gas Station

lawn and down the steps to the sidewalk. I asked if I could help them.

'Mr. Hunt?' The man coming around from the passenger side was talking to me.

"I explained to him I was Bill Hunt.

'Yes, Mr. Hunt.' *He'd said it again*.

"I told him I wasn't used to hearing the Mister part. Told him again I was Bill Hunt and that Mr. Hunt was my father.

'Yes, sir, you are the gentleman I'm looking for. I have something for you.'

"He held out his arm and handed me a large white envelope." *Oh oh, what did I do?*

"The man who gave me the envelope smiled at me. 'No, sir, nothing like that. I was instructed to deliver this to you. Please open it—tell me if it's correct.'

"I felt relieved. I took the envelope and opened it. It contained a government check, a big one. A second piece of paper explained the accounting. It covered all back payments the VA owed me." *Well, kiss my aunt from Savannah!*

"I held onto that check with both hands, just shaking my head. I think my mouth was hanging open. I said nothing.

"The driver finally spoke. 'If that is satisfactory, Mr. Hunt, please sign this receipt—we'll be leaving.'

"I put my John Henry on the receipt, and the first man smiled again. 'Thank you.'

"I told him he was welcome. It sounded so backward."

Chris shook his head in amazement. "And that was it? They left you…with the check?"
"That's what happened." Bill could not stop smiling.
Chris exclaimed—one he had learned from Bill—"Well, I'll be dipped in jelly and rolled."

Bill drove off for Columbia with a fistful of cash for Mrs. Robyn. He returned the next Saturday morning, still smiling, with the rest of the story.
Chris could not wait to hear it. "I guess your landlady was happy to get some money."
Bill answered him. "I told her I had a surprise and handed it to her. Mrs. Robyn took the money and thanked me—but she didn't seem surprised. Then she must've seen the puzzled look on my face and said, 'Well, Bill, I told you I would talk to my old neighbor. You know—the lady whose boy works in Washington, D.C. She called him right away.'
"I thought for a minute, then asked: Who's her boy?
'Why, it's Omar. Omar Bradley.'
"I almost choked—General Omar Bradley?"

I guess even a four-star general is somebody's little boy.

~~

EPILOG

On 22 September, 1950, Omar Bradley was promoted to General of the Army, receiving his fifth star.

He was known as the "Soldier's General."

THE TAIL OF THE LITTLE GRAY-HAIRED LADY

Chris experiences the downside of sophistication.

THE TAIL OF THE
LITTLE GRAY-HAIRED LADY

    On an early afternoon, hot with a cloudless sky, a frisky breeze sent a page of newspaper and an empty Dixie Cup eastward toward the Log Cabin gas station, then—with adequate material available—started a small dust-devil in the intersection of Lucas and Hunt and the Rock Road. Summer was very much in effect.
    By and large, the lunch-hour gasoline customers had been crabby.
    Chris Christopher was working on each of the two islands. He filled the sprinkling cans with water for washing windshields and topping off radiators. He rescued an air hose that had been left lying on the ground and looped it back over its iron reel. Now he wound up the

task of policing the driveways—picking up bottle caps, stray pieces of paper and occasional cigarette butts. Just about finished, he straightened up and glanced at the traffic on St. Charles Rock Road—just in time to see a head-on collision forming.

A black Studebaker had crossed the railroad bridge, westbound and nearing the station lot, when a gray Chevy coupe, eastbound at a high rate of speed, was turning across the westbound lane headed for the gas station driveway. The Studebaker's driver sounded his horn and slammed on the brakes. The driver of the Chevy showed no sign of attempting to avoid anything and continued—still at a high rate—onto the lot. The Studie swerved left, barely clearing the right rear end of the Chevy, then right, to get back into the westbound lane. He continued west, choosing not to stop and exchange pleasantries with the other driver. It turned out to be an excellent choice.

Chris took his double-handful of trash into the office to dump it into the waste paper basket. He turned back to the driveway to service the man behind the wheel of the Chevy coupe. *This guy is crazy*.

The "guy" behind the wheel turned out to be a woman. She exited her vehicle and walked nimbly toward the building. About five feet tall, the woman was oddly constructed. Her upper body—trim, narrow shoulders, slim

The Log Cabin Gas Station

chest—rode atop a voluminous sub-structure that burst forth at the waistline, forming a sphere roughly twice the diameter of her shoulders.

A stylish, small hat was arranged over carefully-coifed steel-gray hair. Although the weather was quite warm she wore a gray jacket that ended at the waist. Her black skirt was hemmed just below the knees, displaying two legs which might have been purchased at Steinway. A small corsage adorned her left lapel.

Noticing Chris waiting for her, she smiled primly and sweetly.

Holy Cow! Some way for a school teacher to be driving.

Chris adjusted to the surprise, returned her smile and waited for her at the door of the station office. More adjustment would soon be in order.

"Did you see that son of a bitch? He was coming right at me—missed me by that much." She held out her hands, palms facing each other, about six inches apart. "I had all I could do to keep him from side-swiping my ass."

Chris rocked back, swallowed, opened and closed his mouth, making no sound. *Tell me this is not coming from the mouth of this little lady.*

Trying to display a sophistication he did not possess, he smiled. "That had to be quite a feat."

She stepped back on one foot, twisted her neck to look up at him and snarled. "Is that supposed to be some kind of personal remark, you little bastard?"

Chris' face went blank. "Fill 'er up?"

She stared coldly into his eyes. He offered a friendly smile.

She continued to glare, silently.

I'd better watch it. This could be trouble.

He dropped his smile. She picked it up. She held it for a second, then clamped her jaw shut.

Chris pumped the gasoline, wiped the windshield and told her the amount of her purchase. She paid the bill and left with no further conversation.

But, the lady must have decided she liked Chris. She became a regular customer for the duration of the summer, returning often for gasoline and staying long enough to talk baseball, current events or the weather.

There was no further mention of the close calls—neither the one on the street nor the one that followed in the driveway.

Several years after his encounter with the gray-haired lady who had side-slipped into the driveway of the Log Cabin Gas Station,

The Log Cabin Gas Station

Chris was working for a totally different employer. He was temporarily assigned to the plant of a large manufacturer of military equipment located near Lambert Municipal Airport. One afternoon he walked into a tool crib in one of the plant buildings.

In the ensuing years there had been changes at the old Log Cabin. A labor strike of long duration had overtaken—and finally compelled—the closing of the chain of gas stations. Chris had been doing a lot of traveling during the intervening years. He had not been aware of the strike or the closing of the stations, but he did recognize the short, gray-haired woman who was working as the tool crib attendant. Chris was genuinely happy to see the old customer he now thought of as an old friend. He approached her smiling, "Hey, it's been a long time."

She looked at him, head tilted, trying to place the face. "I'm not sure I recognize you."

"Oh, maybe you'll remember. You were my customer when I worked at the Log Cabin Gas Station."

The look of concentration on her face slowly evolved into a frown, into a scowl. Growling, she leaped to her feet. Chris noticed a union-employee badge on her jacket lapel.

"Get the hell out of here, Sumbitch. I *never*...in my...*life*—patronized that scab gasoline company!"

Chris left the tool crib without comment.

THESE FOOLISH THINGS

*The reader is taken on a sentimental journey
to the past and
given a preview of things to come.*

THESE FOOLISH THINGS

The afternoon sun made a gleaming beacon of Clayton's handsome Tobler Building. It had been a few years since he'd been back to Missouri and he was now in unfamiliar territory. During his absence, the seat of St. Louis County had grown into a sizeable metro area sporting dozens of large, architecturally pleasing structures. Still, driving into the city from Lambert International, he had no trouble spotting his destination.

Les parked in the garage and entered the lobby from there. The directory in the lobby, located between two of the elevator doors, lists the names and floor numbers of the tenants in levels one through six. To the right, a third elevator door is labeled "Sapient Inquiries - 711." That elevator, alone, travels to the seventh floor, which houses only the offices and residence of Chris Christopher. Les took the elevator on the right.

This afternoon, Chris' secretary Ellen admitted the visitor to her office after he insisted on identifying himself only as "Mr. Les." He had gained an appointment during an earlier phone call when he explained he was an old friend of Chris and wanted his visit to be a bit of a surprise. She knocked once, cracked the door an inch, gave a slight shrug and rolled her eyes heavenward. Chris nodded slightly.

Les entered the room and immediately stopped to look. He found himself in a large office furnished handsomely and decorated tastefully with photos, paintings and a large library area. Ceiling-to-floor windows in each of the four walls provided overviews of Clayton and far into St. Louis County. Chris, his friend of long ago, sat behind a large wooden desk on the side across from the door.

Chris rose, stepped forward, extended his hand, then squinted at the man. Familiar? Maybe. Recognized? No, not yet. Then...

"Les, is it really you? I never thought I'd see you again."

"Sure it's me, who else is this pretty? And what's a few decades between friends?"

He gripped Chris' hand firmly and they shook.

Chris waved a hand toward one of the guest chairs. "How long has it been—20, 25 years? Talk to me. Tell me what you've been doing. Bring me up to date. And to what do I owe this honor?"

"Okay, okay Chris. I just got back to the states, landed noon yesterday in Miami. I had dinner with Denny. We talked old times, of course, and, of course, you got involved in the memories. When Denny told me what you're doing these days I was struck with an idea I haven't been able to shake. Denny told me where I could find you. I took the first flight into town. And let me compliment you on your business and taste in residences."

Les, still looking around, noticed an attractively framed sign on the wall near the door. The sign read, "Have Thesaurus—will obfuscate."

He chuckled. "I guess I'd like to save the story of my life-to-date for later and take the second question first. I want to get something off my chest. Okay with you?"

"Of course, Les. Shoot." Chris returned, to sit behind his desk.

"Fine, I want to begin back in the days of the Log Cabin Gas Station and the Commune...and Ila and me. You remember those times?"

Wincing, Chris tilted his head, leaned back in his chair, legs crossed, feet on the desktop. "I do."

"Fine. I'll start at the beginning." Both men let their minds roll back to the college years....

We have these moments to remember

~~

At one time, on the north side of the old St. Charles Rock Road, west of the suburban city of Wellston, Missouri, there was an ancient log cabin which was first the residence of an early settler and later became the office of an automobile service station. Chris and Les remembered the old place from its second manifestation. Chris worked there, Les was a frequent visitor.

On one particular occasion, business activity at the Log Cabin Gas Station had been slow-to-nonexistent. Les Taylor, driving by, noticed the lull. *A good time for a quick visit with Chris.* He parked near the border fence on the east side of the old cabin.

Les walked around front. Looking through the window, he spotted his friend, feet on the desk, reading a book and smoking a cigarette.

He took the two steps up to the office floor in one stride. "Don't get up. I just came in to have a smoke with you."

"I wasn't planning to get up, and I hope you brought your own smokes."

Les grinned at the typical greeting style of the two friends. "Relax, I have my own. What are you reading?"

"The new Nero Wolfe book." Chris held it up to show the cover. "The title is '*And Be a Villain*'."

"Good?"

"Sure."

Les had no need to disturb Chris' reading. He had just come in for company. He leaned back in the guest chair and smoked for a while in silence. Then—typical for just about any retail business—customers galore! The driveway filled with cars from both directions.

"Huh, figures, I'm here by myself tonight. How about giving me a hand until we get this caught up?"

Chris switched on the power to the West Island pumps as he walked through the door and turned to the right.

Les exited left and walked around the East Island to approach the eastbound car, a large Pontiac sedan, which was now the first of two waiting for service. "Fill it?"

"Nope, just give me 10 gallons."

Les removed the gas cap, positioned it under the lever to keep the nozzle open, inserted the hose nozzle and started the pump. He wet a clean shop towel in the water bucket, took a dry one from a shelf and began to clean the windshield.

Oh my, this deserves a closer look. He stepped around to the rear door of the sedan and began to remove an imaginary smear on the glass. The young Chinese man who sat against the far side of the rear seat was Frank Lee. He and Les had been friends throughout high school. The younger man who sat nearest to the window that Les was rubbing was Frank's younger brother, Tom. The gorgeous young woman in the middle seat now occupied Les' complete attention. However, if she knew he was there, it was not apparent. Les continued to polish the same spot on the window.

Her brother was not unaware. Frank growled something under his breath; Denny, the driver, heard the command and started the engine. Les, jarred from his hypnotic trance, stopped wiping the window and grabbed for the gas hose. Denny handed even money, a dollar and some coins, through the window and drove off.

"Chris, who the hell *was* that? She's lovely."

"Oh, yeah, she's Frank's and Tommy's sister. Nice girl, very sharp, very talented."

"Talented, huh? What's her name?"

"What am I...an encyclopedia? Her name's Ila. Comes from her Chinese name: Ah-EE. It means `Lovely.'"

"Jeez, I'll say! Tell me she's not married."

The Log Cabin Gas Station

"Nope, had an affair, didn't work well, back living at the commune."

"Commune?"

Chris explained that he and three or four other people rented rooms from Frank Lee. Frank, being the oldest brother, had inherited his parent's house. The house was fairly large, having five bedrooms, the largest of which Frank reserved for himself. The others, all of them friends, were welcome to stay in any available area for however long, so long as they "behave like gentlemen". They were to help maintain the property and obtain food to be shared. Frank's sister Ila and brother Tommy were permanent guests.

Frank owned the house outright, there was no mortgage. This communal relationship had been working well and those who lived there referred to their home as The Commune.

"Chris, can I rent a room in The Commune?" The whole idea sounded good to Les—and *she* lived there.

Chris asked Frank and Les was in luck.

That very day Frank had accepted a long-term assignment to some unnamed location and within a week he had moved out of his bedroom. Ila claimed rights to it since it was the best and warmest room in the house and Les moved into Ila's former room.

There's no substitute for good luck. Within no time at all Les and Ila had become friends and then good friends—but—nonetheless—just friends.

Les learned that—in addition to being a beautiful young woman—Ila was a talented dancer and singer. Her voice, in a naturally low register, was soft and sweet. Her repertoire included just about all of the popular love songs of the last several years. In front of any of the numerous dance-bands in the Normandy, Pine Lawn and Wellston areas she was a crowd pleaser. Les loved to hear her sing and he knew the Billy Eckstein trademark to be a favorite of hers. Secretly he treasured the fact that it described his own thoughts so well.

I reached for you like I'd reach for a star

~~

Then one chilly night, Les' luck worked again. It was Friday evening and Ila had gone for an all-weekend stay with a couple of girlfriends. During the night, the outside temperature dropped like a rock and the bedrooms became cold or colder. His was the coldest of all.

About four in the morning he remembered that Frank's bedroom was right above the furnace and that it always stayed fairly warm. Of course Frank's room was now the turf of Ila—but she was gone for the weekend. A survivor by nature, Les migrated quietly into Ila's bedroom, rolled up close to the wall and immediately fell asleep.

Later he recalled being somewhat aware of someone else joining him on the other side of the bed—another survivor, probably Chris, maybe Denny, but he was willing to share and went right back to sleep.

Then came daybreak, with Les finding himself being kicked, pummeled and screamed at. Fists and feet were coming in like hail stones on a high wind.

"Get the hell out of my bed, Dummy." Ila had returned.

He climbed over her—kicks still coming strong— and headed for the door and his room.

Over his shoulder, "I'll apologize later."

By breakfast, cooler heads prevailed and they were ready to laugh it off.

By dinner, they began to wonder what they might have missed. And each one knew the other was thinking likewise. They did not wait for the next cold night to find out.

Since this is the perfect spot to learn, teach me tonight.

~~

Les was not a virgin. But he had a lot to learn. The idea that at least 51 per cent of satisfaction came from the knowledge that one had satisfied his partner was not in his ken. The typically short and sweet performances of the teenage male made anything approaching physical satisfaction for the woman a rare experience—rare to mythical.

Now, Les had acquired enough experience to know when a partner's participation had failed to fulfill. Truth be known, the fact wasn't always that important. But he really cared about Ila and he knew it hadn't been enough for her. Still, he was spent for the moment and time was of the essence. Someone would be coming home soon. Another opportunity would not appear this night.

With just a few minutes left he began to slide down her body, to do for her something he had only recently read about. His lips had reached her belly when Ila murmured, "What are you doing?"

He froze. *Why did she ask? Did she not want it?* He stopped.

She was silent for a long moment, then: "Tell me you love me."

A longer silence while he mustered his courage. His mind said, "I have loved you since I first saw you that night in the car." He had never said words like that to anyone. His voice could not produce a coherent rendition of what his heart and mind were telling him to say.

"Les...?"

Rambling, almost stuttering, he uttered, "It has been...so long that I have loved you." There. He had gotten it out. He sighed.

Those stumbling words that told you what my heart meant.

Or not.

~~

He felt her body tense. He misread it. *Was she ready for more?*
"You didn't have to say that." Her tone was flat, crisp.
He relaxed. He imagined that, not only had he satisfied her request, he'd surprised her with an overstatement. *But, since she liked it...I know I pleased her*.
She went to her bedroom. They talked no more that night.
"Chris, I was so damn green.
"The next morning I went back to college. We wrote a couple of notes, back and forth, you know, but she never seemed to have anything of substance to say. There was no evidence that she felt our love had been important, that there should have been more.
I couldn't understand, but I knew I shouldn't persist. I stopped writing.
"I graduated, began a good career, traveled a lot. I've never had time to think

about marriage. There have been other women, but Ila was never, ever, completely out of my mind.

"Chris, I've never forgotten her."

Careless, now that you've got me loving you...

~~

"Then one evening, years later, on the road, the TV was off, the radio was on, and damned if they didn't play *Careless*. That song had been popular at the time of Ila and me. I had liked to hear her sing it, along with others she did so beautifully. If she ever intended there to be any hidden meaning, I never picked up on it.

"That night, the song sharpened my attention. Memory—as never before—brought back the details, the words we said to each other that night. Was it possible I'd said something that disappointed her?

"I recalled what I meant to say, and...what I...did...say. Oh, DAMN!"

*Falling in love with love
is falling for make-believe*

~~

In his own opinion, Chris felt that Les had far overestimated the severity of his clumsy response to Ila. Nevertheless, over the many years, it had become a fact of Les' life. Certainly there was no way he, Chris, felt qualified—or motivated—to try to disabuse Les of his burden.

Anguished, Les said, "I would never have hurt her intentionally, but I know I did hurt her...*now* I know. I wanted to tell her. I had no idea where she was, how to communicate. Then last night I learned that you were still here in the area, and about your business. I thought you might know how to find her—to be able to help me."

Behind his desk, Chris leaned back in his chair, sat gazing into the past and said nothing. He remembered other love-stricken young men—high school, early college years, even in the military—with the same reaction to "Puppy-Love", "Young Love-True Love."

He'd always worked on keeping his distance from these guys and their problems. Sooner or later they all got over it. Evidently all but one. Now it seemed he had a throw-back in his office.

Then—after several minutes went by—Les broke the silence. "Chris, are you still with me?"

Chris snapped back to attention. "I'm sorry. You had me lost in the past. You really mean this—it's still important to you?"

"I think of her—and what I said to her—and I can't get it off my mind. I want to find her and somehow explain. It's a debt...it needs to be paid."

Chris sucked in a deep breath and let it out slowly.

"I'll get your message to her, but I'll want no questions from you and you'll get no answers from me. Does that work for you?" Chris would not be party to disturbing the life of a woman who almost certainly was enjoying living in the present.

Les looked at him quizzically and thought about it. "Well, okay, that will have to work."

Opening a desk drawer, Chris took a piece of blank stationary, pushed it across the desk to Les, handed him a pen. "Write your message to her so she'll know they are your words. I don't want to make a mistake on my end."

His client held the pen, stared at the paper for a short while and wrote slowly, carefully for several minutes. Chris read it, nodded, slid it into an envelope and sealed it.

He got to his feet, came around the desk, and removed a bottle of Crown Royal and two lowball glasses from the credenza. He poured two drinks, handed one to Les. "It's good to see you again. I'll get on this myself, right away, and let you know just as soon as I get it done."

They finished their drinks. Les stood and moved toward the office door. Chris rose, followed him and opened the door.

Les grabbed Chris' hand, pumped it. "Old friend...thanks so much for talking with me. I hope you know how much I appreciate this."

Ten days later Ellen scheduled Les Taylor's next appointment. Les entered, accepted a seat. Apprehensive.

"Relax, man, I have a report for you." Chris saw his friend working on being stoic.

"Your note has been delivered and placed in her hands."

"Man, you did it! You found her!" He came half out of his seat, leaned forward, eyes fixed on Chris, attentive, expectant. "Did she read it? What did she say?"

Chris looked his guest in the eye. "Do you remember the rules? No questions... no answers?"

"Chris, you've got to be kidding. I need to know." *What's with him?*

"Why the secrecy?"

"Les—let me give you this: Your note was clear and most considerate. You have no reason to be apprehensive."

Les' face relaxed. He sighed and sank back in his chair.

"A couple more things I can tell you: her last name is no longer Lee—shouldn't be a surprise. She has been living in Las Vegas for a lot of years. She is a kind, thoughtful woman. She is well."

Les showed his astonishment. "Las Vegas? My Lord. I've been there often. Actually lived and worked there for a short time. I never knew."

He shook his head slowly, silently absorbing the reality, contemplating fickle fortune.

Chris watched him steadily with no comment.

Les took the deepest of breaths, sighed, turned to Chris. "Buddy, I owe you big-time. What's the tariff?"

"It's on the house...no, wait! Buy me a drink. There's a great bar downstairs, right off the lobby."

Sing the Whiffenpoofs assembled, with their glasses raised on high,
and the magic of their singing casts its spell...

~~

PARTYING
IS
SUCH SWEET SORROW

*Chris attends an unexpected party
and soon after is a no-show
at one where he is to be
the guest of honor.*

PARTYING IS SUCH SWEET SORROW

  Shortly after the time of purchase, just about every car is endowed by its new owner with a personality—and usually a name and gender. The recognition as an entity then grows in the mind of the owner—and thus in the deepest hidden parts of its electronics—until the device becomes a trustee, and then a friend, and then a member of the family.
  The wonderful relationship deepens and solidifies until that sad moment when the owner must come to the realization that it is time for friends to part.
  Even as he has received his last ride from his trusted friend, the seller often feels it necessary to deliver a eulogy in the presence

of the buyer—words that fall also upon the departed.

"Yep, Old Red has been a good and reliable worker."

"Oh she's been such a honey...I'm going to miss her."

But once it is sold, the car's spirit dies. The former owner turns and looks back at the grill of his old friend and sees, no longer, the familiar grinning face but a lifeless pair of glass eyes. He walks away with the dealer to the other side of the lot where the newer, shinier models are for sale. What remains of the old friend now rests among the others in the bone yard.

The two owners of the used car lots in the following story knew these truths. They would tell of not-infrequent return trips by a past owner who came to view, for one more time, the car he had sold.

They also knew—from much experience—that the best way to lose a potential buyer is to offend, by bad-mouthing, the car he had just sold. And these two knew about dealing in used cars.

~~

Somewhere in the unfathomable geography of South St. Louis, along Grand Boulevard (ubiquitously called by the denizens "Grand Avenue") there were two used car lots positioned side-by-side. The lots were so closely adjacent that no one but a surveyor would be able to tell you where they began and ended. Further, the merchandise was positioned for the mutual convenience of the two proprietors, and often one's car would be parked on the other's lot.

This was fine with Mike Spengler and Lou Sorkin. They knew which cars they owned. And often, when one or the other needed or wanted to be gone from his lot, the dealer who remained on duty would sell any car on either lot. The residual finances were always handled without ever a bump.

Although a fairly large used-car lot, Mike Spengler's was the smaller of the two. Containing a more selective stock of merchandise, for the most part the cars were all later models in good or spotless conditions.

The sprawling lot of Lou Sorkin was far more of an *olla podrida colecion*. Up front, a finer selection of quality, style and condition was not to be found on the south side. But as the buyer strolled deeper among the vintage cars, he would find a plentiful number of older vehicles in a wide range of condition and utility. These were of value more to the curious and the collector than to a man who needed something to get himself and the family to and from.

One standout in the group was a 1933 Duesenberg SJ, a marvelous metal monster that—had it been in different condition—would have commanded a king's ransom from a well-heeled buyer who might want to show off his taste and wealth. That is, *if* the above and *if* Sorkin had had a title to the vehicle. Lou swore to anyone who would listen, he did not know how the car got there. A few years earlier when he came in to begin the work day, there she sat, up near the street, looking unlike anything else on the lot.

Lou left the car where it was parked and went into the office, figuring the owner would be by later to talk about a sale or trade. That didn't happen.

A busy man, Sorkin didn't even approach the car for a day or two. He had more immediate profit-centered matters to handle. Finally, three or four days later he turned his attention to the still-unclaimed beast on display in the "Better Cars" section of the lot.

Walking up to the car, he half-expected to find locked doors—not so. He opened the driver's-side door and poked his head inside for a preliminary look. The overwhelming smell of death inside the sun-baked car knocked him back and almost down. Reeling, he staggered away from the car, then more purposefully toward the shade-side of his office building. He leaned against the wall and breathed deeply of

The Log Cabin Gas Station

cooler, cleaner air. "Oh shit! Oh shit, shit, shit, shit, DAMN!"

A tentative explanation for the arrival of the car was forming in his mind. It was not welcome.

What must he do? What next? He needed more facts before he could come up with a plan of action. He forced himself to walk back to the car. The door was still open.

The seats were unoccupied; there was nothing (or "Oh God—no one") on the floor. He slammed the door closed.

The absolute last thing that he wanted to face up to was the thing he needed to do next. He walked to the rear of the vehicle. Tried the trunk lid. Lifted it very slightly. It was unlocked. He snatched his hand away and the lid dropped closed.

Standing there, trying to focus his thoughts, he caught himself wringing his hands in lieu of positive action. *Come on, Pussy, open the fucking trunk!* He resisted his own command, then looked around to see if anyone was watching. He forced himself to open the trunk. He reached for the lid and flung it open. The trunk was empty! Nothing! *Nada!*

Feeling stronger and more aggressive now, he walked around the car, taking more careful notice of its appearance. He found several suspicious holes—maybe about 45 caliber holes—not only in the trunk but in the rear fenders. None in any window.

Time to call the police.

By the time the policeman arrived, it was the middle of a hot, humid morning. The copper had sent to another assignment before his breakfast that morning, then after completing the early job was told to beat feet immediately to the car lot. Lou's description of his find required an immediate checkout.

Lou directed the copper to the car, pointed to the driver's door. The policeman opened the door and caught a whiff that he'd smelled often enough before. He backed away and made a note in a book he carried. Not closing the car door, he walked around the front and opened the right-hand door. "Yep, somebody's dead somewhere."

The policeman checked the trunk, under the hood and then made a comprehensive, although quick, survey of the rest of the car. He commented, "Someone picked up all the slugs," and made another note. He noted the absence of license plates.

He turned to Lou Sorkin, asked permission to use the phone, made a call and made more notes.

Then, "Sir, Headquarters says we've had no report of a vehicle meeting the description of this one having been stolen or involved in anything illegal. I feel sure that we will soon. I'd suggest you put this car somewhere where it can be found when and if we need it. Until then, I have no reason to have the car taken in.

"Thank you for calling us. Have a good day." He sat in his own car and made another note. He threw a sort-of salute to Lou and drove off.

Lou heard nothing further in the following years. He had the car moved to its present spot in the back of the lot. He began to show the car to interested buyers, but since it never lost all the smell and since he did not have a title, he didn't pursue a sale.

The office of the Spengler lot was a small white frame building that sat on the far back corner. Sorkin's office was positioned near the border line and close to the street. It was also a white frame building, considerably larger than Spengler's, and most frequently occupied by both dealers and whatever friends of either happened to be visiting. And, the spaciousness of the building made it perfect for hosting the regular Friday night crap game. Bill Hunt recently brought Chris Christopher into the group, introducing him as, "My friend from the gas station."

In what appeared to be a rite of initiation, Chris was taken to the back lot and introduced to the Duesenberg. Perhaps since he owned his own relic, Chris did not make an offer.

The crap games were well attended, usually by a half-dozen or so of regular players, a congenial group of young men who enjoyed the game and each other. Each would be armed with his own six-pack and, usually, his own pair of dice. The spacious floor of the office was cleared for the play. The players sat on the floor, leaning against the walls. They would participate—or just watch—at their own choice, as the game proceeded through the evening. A comfortable amount of cash changed hands during the evenings, but week after week the winnings seemed to level out fairly well.

A good time was always had by all.

One evening, about 90 minutes into the game, Chris had just finished a roll.
He had been using his own pair of dice—a red-colored clear pair—when Mike moved forward and reached for the dice.

Then—loudly—"Hey y'all! This is going to be a Private Roll. Just me and Lou. All others back off!"

This was unusual. He got immediate attention and silence in the room.

Mike continued, "The bet on this roll is simple—Lou and I each put up our car lots! Winner takes all!"

"Yeah."

"Sure."

"Be serious, you guys."

The Log Cabin Gas Station

"Come on."

"What the fuck." Murmurs from around the walls.

"Okay you all, quiet and stay clear. This *is* serious." Mike spoke in a low but firm tone. He raised Chris' dice and got ready to shoot.

A snarl came from Lou, "All right! Dammit... I see you knuckling those dice. Hell, I've been watching you all evening."

Mike came right back at him. "Well don't think I haven't watched you...Ring-fingering...your share of the time."

At this, both men reached behind themselves. Two pistols came out of nowhere. The room burst into action—players ducked under desks, chairs, into the restroom.

The room went dark. Two shots rang out...then silence...a deathly silence that seemed to last and last.

The smell of cordite filled the room. Then the sound of laughter.

The lights came on, the players opened their eyes to see Lou and Mike grinning, hugging, and pointing to two bullet holes in the ceiling.

Bill Hunt spoke first." What the flock do you ignomooses think you're doing?" Bill loved to toy with the language, often to ease tension.

Mike returned Chris' dice. Then he explained. He had decided to go west, to join the burgeoning activity in search of uranium ore. "Lou will be managing both lots until I make it or break it in the desert."

The room relaxed. Smiles and head-shaking replaced the tension. Lou made a phone call. In a few minutes a panel-delivery truck—obviously stationed nearby—rolled up with a cargo of several dozen White Castles and a cask of Stag.

The farewell party for Mike was in full swing.

EPILOG

Time passed. Mike formed a mining company with investments from his friends. He bought a worthless mine site, worked hard and went broke.

On his second try he hit it big. Mike and his backers became very wealthy.

One day Lou had had enough. He arranged to have the Duesenberg towed away, to a junkyard in Jennings.

~~

Meanwhile, far to the west in Wellston, the denizens of The Commune were putting the finishing touches on *The Party For Chris*. The popular Chris Christopher—when he was in town—was the de facto head of the household, being close-to-the-oldest male, nearly the tenant of longest tenure, and by reason of possessing the bulk of experience-derived maturity.

Earlier in the year, Frank Lee had received a sudden call to duty. Given the time to think about it, Frank would have picked Chris as his deputy.

Chris was a friend to all, a capable and fair umpire, a goal-stter and decision- maker. He taught ethics by example, while being loose enough to be fun.

When he was gone, Frank's sister, Ila, a stunning young woman who also possessed the necessary leadership skills, guided The Commune.

In addition, she had no travel plans.

Whatever—Chris would be home from college in Decatur during the Christmas holidays. He was a good guy, and that called for a party.

~~

"Okay, he says he'll be in on the 17th. The 18th is a Saturday. We'll do it then. That gives us a week to get this place looking clean and decent. Not much time, but we can do it. Let's get with it!"

Ila had spoken. Now, with a couple of days to spare, all was as ready as it needed to be. Dates were invited, food—including treats from the Jewish deli and bakery—was ordered, phono records located or borrowed. Crepe paper streamers were twisted and thumb-tacked into the corners of the living room. Bedrooms were made decent in optimistic expectations of getting lucky.

Ila had her special treats taken care of: a box of *Parliament English Ovals* stashed away, and the ingredients for her specialty, *Stuffed Cabbage Leaves,* in the fridge. *This will be so fine!*

Late on the morning of Thursday, December 16th, Dean was alone at the house. The radio was on, Ed Wilson was spinning tunes. Dean heard what he thought might be the sound of Chris' Model A in front of the house. It didn't figure to be, but he got up to check it anyway. The engine sound died; Dean watched as Chris got out and started up the steps. "What are you doing here a day early? Party's not 'til tomorrow."

Chris looked glum...very. "Dean, things have changed. I'm in a hurry and I need your help. I'll be calling a cab in a little while. I'll get a few things from my room and ask you to keep or pitch the rest. Or pass it along. Sell my car and hold the money until the next time I see you. Come to think of it...take it to Lou Sorkin's lot on Grand. Tell him you're selling it for me."

Dean looked at Chris questioningly but said nothing. They had been close friends for a long time.

"I'm okay, Dean. It's just that I've taken a new job and need to be away for a while. I'm to connect with no one, for the time being. I can't answer questions, so please don't ask. Please apologize to everybody. Tell them I'm really sorry that I have to miss my own party and I hope they have a great time."

Dean looked at Chris for a moment. "Okay" was all he said. Then Chris was gone.

~~

"Well hell...we'll do one in his honor." No party would be canceled for something as ethereal as the strange defection of Chris. Dean's recital of Chris' parting words—with numerous curtain calls—nourished conversations, conjectures, and hypotheses during the early part of the evening. Dean himself declined steadfastly to deviate from, or amplify upon, the original text.

Optimists all, the denizens were certain they'd see the man again.

Ila walked slowly into her bedroom. Brought out an *English Oval*. Slumped into the armchair in the living room. Lit the cigarette. Sat smoking and looking past the living room,

Hal D. Simpkin

and the dining room, at something a very long way away.

THE BEGINNING . . .

~~

I'm happy to know you enjoyed **The Log Cabin Gas Station**. Want to know why Chris missed his party?

His story continues in the book **G-Eye**—right after World War II—when America faced the spread of World Communism and the U.S. Army dedicated an undercover unit to help the FBI expose and counter that threat.

The FBI became aware of a subversive two-pronged attack on our country: Following the war, the United States possessed the only functioning industrial capability in the world. Devoid of engineering and manufacturing know-how, the Soviets immediately began a broad-side espionage effort to infiltrate our industrial plants designed to plunder America's knowledge and skills.

Close behind this peril the Communists crafted the infiltration of our schools with socialist-oriented teachers and college professors. They were given a mission of implanting the doctrine of Soviet Bolshevism in the receptive young minds of our children.

The targets of the espionage were many. FBI manpower was severely limited. A plan was devised for the Army to recruit and train qualified counter-intelligence personnel to uncover and report—to the FBI—all subversive

Hal D. Simpkin

activity. The mandate was not in the traditional scope of the Army. Heavy resistance in Congress was predictable. Any resultant publicity would destroy the plan. But the task was vital, and the decision to proceed was made when the Army and a few Senators with the appropriate noesis agreed to support the plan—without further disclosure.

Get a copy of **G-Eye** and follow Chris Christopher and the adventure.

To purchase a copy of The Log Cabin Gas Station, visit www.mirasmartshop.com, www.allonthesamepagebookstore.com, or AbeBooks.com.

The Log Cabin Gas Station

From *G-Eye:*

Terry interrupted his talk. Removed his glasses. Gazed, reflecting, over our heads. Brought his eyes down, looked at each of us briefly, and resumed. "You know, when this ruckus between Moscow and Washington began, for a while I tended to feel the same way. Why are we doing this? I no longer wonder." He moved his eyes along the line of ours. "If any of you have a notion that the Communists are our friends . . . get over it. They are not. They are our deadly enemies."

~~

Americans began to understand that the problem was real, that our way of life was at stake. For the duration of the war the Russians, of necessity, had allied themselves with the West. But, as the exigencies of winning the war against Hitler's Nazis faded from memory, the Soviet Union exposed its own plans for the future of the world. Their plans included no less than converting the world to the rule of Communism.

Feel the nostalgia of post-war America.
Recall the Communist threat.
Solve the secret of Daisy.
READ *G-Eye.*

Hal D. Simpkin

Hal D. Simpkin has a M.S. degree in Business Management from Lindenwood University, with undergraduate work done at the University of Missouri, St. Louis. His two full-time employers were the United States Army and McDonnell Aircraft Corporation in St. Louis, Mo. where he was a member of the Flight Test Division.

His first novel, *G-Eye,* was published by High Hill Press in 2009. Recently, his short story *Road to the World,* a memoir, was selected by the St. Louis Writers Guild for their anthology *St. Louis Reflections,* honoring its 90th anniversary.

He and his wife live in Missouri.